JOKER

Kathy Lee

Each *Seasiders* story is complete in itself – but if you enjoy this book, you may like to read the others in the series:

Runners

Liar

Winner

The same people (plus some new ones!) appear in all the books.

Scripture Union

Leave all your worries with God, because he cares for you.
(1 Peter 5 verse 7, from the *Good News Bible*)

© Kathy Lee 2000
First Published 2000

Scripture Union, 207–209 Queensway, Bletchley, Milton Keynes
MK2 2EB, England

ISBN 1 85999 358 3

British Library Cataloguing-in-Publication Data.
A catalogue record of this book is available from the British
Library.

Printed and bound in Great Britain by Cox & Wyman Ltd,
Reading.

Chapter 1

Who got the sack on his very first day at work?

The postman.

When I got home from school, Dad's car was outside the front door. That was the first strange thing. He should be at work – why was he home so early?

The second strange thing: where was Mum? Our dog Jerry came to meet me in the hall, wagging his tail frantically, over-excited like a five-year-old on Christmas Day. (Well, five-year-olds don't normally wag their tails, but you know what I mean.)

But no one called from the kitchen, "Hi, Ben. Is that you?" That's what Mum always said.

"How do you know it's me?" I asked her once. "It could be Grace or Hannah."

"They're not as noisy as you," she said.

"So if you know it's me, why do you say *Is that you*? Who else are you expecting that's noisy – King Kong? Attila the Hun?"

That reminded me of a joke. What's wild and ferocious and covered in icing? Answer: Attila the Bun. But it was no good telling it just then, because I'd given away the punchline. Anyway, Mum had heard all my jokes before. (Probably hundreds of times before.)

It was nice having a mum who was usually there when I got home. But where was she today? I dropped my bag on the floor and went into the kitchen. Nobody there apart from Tubs, our big fat tabby, who was asleep on a window-sill. The back door was open, though. I could hear voices from the garden… angry voices. And that was the strangest thing of all. It sounded as if Mum and Dad were having an argument.

How weird! I knew that some people's parents had rows. Some people's parents even fought each other, or got divorced and never spoke to each other again. I had never heard *my* parents arguing, though. Mum used to say that in fifteen years of marriage, they hadn't had one angry word.

But they were certainly arguing now.

"Why didn't you *tell* me?" Mum was saying crossly. "Why didn't you give me a bit of warning? I wouldn't have booked us that holiday if I'd known."

Dad muttered something about not wanting to worry her, in case it never happened.

"How long ago did you find out?"

"Not till today – not for certain. But there's been rumours going about for a few weeks."

"A few weeks? You should have told me! I could have taken up that offer of a full-time job. I would have done, if only I'd known."

Dad said, "Part-time, full-time, makes no difference. We can't possibly live on what you earn – you know we can't. They only pay you peanuts."

"Peanuts is better than nothing at all!" She was really angry now. She was fond of her job, working part-time in a day nursery. (I think she would have liked it if my sisters and I had stopped growing at about age three.)

I went out into the garden. Mum and Dad looked surprised and… sort of guilty. They didn't want me to know they had been quarrelling, I could tell.

Dad forced a smile, and Mum said, out of habit, "Hi, Ben. Is that you? I didn't realise what the time was."

"What's the matter?" I asked.

They looked at each other. Dad said, "Well, he'll have to know, won't he?"

"Know what?"

"I'm out of a job. Cuthberts have gone bust."

I had sort of guessed it already. After all, it had happened before, a couple of years ago. Another building firm had gone bankrupt; Dad had been out of work for months. But we had managed all right, hadn't we? Money had been tight for a while, but no one had starved to death, not even Tubs. (Especially not Tubs. On a desert island, Tubs would probably outlive all the rest of us.)

"What's so bad about it?" I said. "You never liked it much at Cuthberts. Maybe the next job will be better."

"If there is a next job," Dad said gloomily. "Why d'you think I stayed on at Cuthberts, even though I hated it?"

"I don't know."

"Because I was lucky to get that job. There was nothing else around two years ago and there's even less now. The building trade's deep in trouble. Do you know what 'recession' means?"

I shook my head.

"It means there's not much work around. Nobody's buying houses, they haven't the money. Cuthberts couldn't sell that last lot we built – half of them are still standing empty. And it's the same with every building firm in the area."

"So you might be out of work for a long time?" I said. Dad said, "Yes."

"Well, we hope not," Mum said brightly. "We'll have to see what turns up."

All at once Jerry shot indoors. Hannah or Grace must have come home – if it was a stranger, he would have barked his head off.

It was both of them. Hannah is fourteen, three years older than me, and Grace is nine. In one way they look alike, both small for their age, with fair, curly hair like Mum's. (I am more like Dad, quite tall and dark.)

In another way, Hannah and Grace are very different. They look like the Before and After pictures in one of Mum's magazines. 'Before' is Hannah, looking bored and fed-up with life. 'After' is Grace – much better-looking, not because of make-up or a haircut, but because she's smiling. Hannah could look nice too, only she can't be bothered most of the time.

Hannah was all right until a couple of years ago, when she suddenly became a teenager instead of a normal person. "She'll grow out of it one day," Mum says. "Well, we can always hope."

When she heard about Dad's job, Hannah looked more sulky than ever. "Oh, great," she muttered. "I suppose that means no pocket money for months and months, and no new clothes." (Typical. She only ever thinks about herself.)

Grace looked frightened for a moment. Then she said, "But it will be all right, won't it Mum? We can pray about it."

Mum smiled down at her. "Yes, love, of course we can."

I thought of what Andy had said at the church Youth Club. (He's the assistant minister, but he's a really good laugh. I like him.) He had read a verse from the Bible: *My times are in God's hands.*

"Notice this," he said. "It doesn't say which times. Good times or bad times – we're all going to have times in our lives when we feel great, and other times when we feel like taking a walk off the end of the pier. But it doesn't matter. Good times or bad times, sick or healthy, rich or poor, Deep Pan Pizza or school dinner stew… it doesn't matter. My times are in God's hands – and they are hands that love me and care for me."

He stopped then, because some of the kids were getting restless. They had come to play football, not to be preached at.

So I never got the chance to ask the question that had begun to bother me. If God really loves us, why do bad times happen at all? Why isn't life smooth and easy and happy, like a great big bowl of ice cream?

And now Dad had lost his job. Bad times were on the way – any idiot could see that. Even the dog, whining softly and nosing my hand, could tell that something was wrong.

I have a great memory for jokes. I know a joke for every occasion, every sport, every job, every animal or bird or fish. But somehow, at that moment, not one joke came to mind. Not a single one.

Chapter 2

Why did the old lady have her hair in a bun?

Because she had her teeth in a cheeseburger.

Mum cancelled our holiday in Spain. She said we just couldn't afford it.

"Don't we get a holiday at all, then?" Hannah wailed, although at the time when Mum was booking it, she'd made a huge fuss. (She didn't want to go on holiday with her stupid family, she said.)

"Of course we'll have some kind of holiday," said Mum. "We can always go camping – that's nice and cheap."

Hannah said, "Yuk! I hate camping. It rains all the time and there's never anything to do, except go on stupid walks or sit on stupid beaches. If I wanted to do that, which I don't, I could do it here in Westhaven."

"At least it would be a different beach," Mum said mildly. "Change of scenery. And we could go to somewhere like Bournemouth, where there's more for you to do."

Westhaven, where we live, is a seaside town, but not a huge one. It has a pier, a harbour, a fun-fair, and loads of hotels. In summer it gets quite busy; in winter it goes as quiet as an empty church. But winter or summer, Hannah's always moaning about how boring it is.

We live in quite an old part of town – Fountain Square. Dad says our house is 180 years old. When we moved in, years ago, it was in a terrible state, but Dad has slowly been doing it up. Most of it is really nice now. It's tall and thin, four storeys high – five if you count the basement. Mum often grumbles about all the stairs, and says why don't we move to a bungalow? (She doesn't really mean it.)

I have my own big room on the second floor, looking out on the trees in the Square. On the opposite side is a hotel called Sea View, which is made from three houses the size of ours, all knocked together. My friend Jake lives there; his family runs the place. Jake and I have always been friends, even though he's in the year above me at school.

Jake doesn't much like living in a hotel. Well, it's hard work, especially at the height of the season. Sea View would soon be crammed with Piggies (that's what Jake calls the summer visitors, and their children are the Piglets). At busy times, Jake and his brother would have to help with the work; they would earn lots of extra money but have very little time to spend it. And *they* wouldn't be going on holiday – not until about November.

When I told him Dad was out of work, Jake said, "Huh. I wish that would happen to my Dad."

"You don't really," I said.

"Yes I do. I've hardly talked to him for days. He's either working, or so tired that all he wants to do is snooze in front of the telly. At least your dad has got time to do things with you and take you out."

"Yeah, well soon we won't be able to afford to go out. Anything like that costs money." This reminded me of a joke. "What does a mean person do when the weather turns cold?"

"I dunno," said Jake. "What *does* a mean person do when the weather turns cold?"

"Sit next to a candle. And what does he do when it turns absolutely freezing?…Light the candle."

Jake made a face. "At least," he said, "things can't be too bad if you're still telling jokes."

"It's like my grandad says. You have to laugh, or else you'd cry."

My granny and grandad live not far away, in a block of old people's flats. They haven't always lived there. (Well, naturally. They haven't always been old people.)

I can remember, before Granny got ill, when they didn't seem old at all. We used to go and visit them in their house at Barcliff. It had a wonderful garden that ran to the edge of the cliff. Granny was always worried that one of us kids would fall over the edge, so Grandad put up a good strong fence.

But in the end it was Granny herself who was in danger. Her mind was starting to go. Sometimes, when we went to see her, she would be quite okay; other times she would act very strangely. She wouldn't want to talk to us. She seemed to have forgotten who we were.

"What's wrong with Granny?" I remember asking, when I was about eight. "I don't think I like her any more."

Mum sighed. "She's ill, that's what it is. Ill in her mind."

"When will she get better?"

"It's not that kind of illness. It's called Alzheimer's disease. Once people get it, they never really get better – not until they're in Heaven."

I didn't believe her. I wanted Granny to get better – to be like the Granny I remembered. So for weeks and weeks I prayed about it, but nothing happened. She was getting worse, not better.

Early one morning, the Barcliff milkman found Granny wandering the street in her nightie. She must have managed to unlock the front door while Grandad was still asleep. "It's a mercy she went out the front and not the back," Grandad said, thinking of the cliff-top. "The sooner we move out of here, the better."

So they had moved into a flat in Westhaven, near the park. It was only five minutes away; Mum often popped in to visit them. Hannah, Grace and I went less often, because Granny was very odd these days.

Grandad had changed too. He didn't smile much any more. He looked very tired; Granny often woke him up in the middle of the night.

"It can be pitch dark outside," he said, "but there she is, struggling to get up and dress herself. 'We'll be late, we'll be late,' she mutters, but when I say 'late for what?' she doesn't know."

I looked at Granny. She had nodded off in her arm-chair, snoring quietly. She seemed about ninety years old, although I knew she was only 65, the same age as Grandad.

Mum said, "Maybe if we kept her awake in the day-time she'd sleep better at night."

"You try, then," said Grandad wearily. "Easier said than done."

Mum tried to wake her up, but she wasn't having it. Even when Mum was talking to her, her eyes kept closing. Grandad shook her by the arm, and she swiped him away like a fly. "Lemealone. Tired," she mumbled. "Seeyoumorrow."

"The trouble is, tomorrow for Winnie is the middle of the night for me," said Grandad.

"You can't go on like this," said Mum. "Maybe it's time to think about –"

"No! I won't have her put in a home," Grandad said fiercely. "Over my dead body!"

"All right, all right," Mum soothed him. "But at least let me give you a good night's sleep now and then. I'll spend the night here and you can stop at our place."

So once or twice a week it was Dad who woke us in the morning and got us our breakfast. He wasn't as good at it as Mum. He couldn't find the marmalade, or the lunch boxes, or my games kit. If we complained, he told us to be quiet because Grandad was asleep upstairs. It was a real pain.

"I wish they *would* put Granny in a home," Hannah muttered, "She's a nuisance to everybody."

"Takes one to know one," I said. "You're a nuisance to everybody, so why don't we put you in a home?"

"Because no place would take you," said Dad. "Come on, kids, get out that door. You're late."

Chapter 3

Here is the six o clock news:

Hundreds of wigs have been stolen from a factory in Wigan.

Police are combing the area

"What's that banging noise?" asked Jake.

We had been kicking a football about in the middle of the Square, but now that we'd stopped, we could hear the sound of furious hammering. It came from our basement.

"It's Dad," I said.

"Oh. Your mum's locked him up again, has she?"

"No, he's working. I don't mean paid work – he's making a separate flat in our basement. Then we might rent it out and make some money."

This was only part of his reason for doing it. I knew he hated having no work to do – that was why he'd started on the basement. Anything was better than just sitting around.

It didn't help that Mum was working full-time. She used to work only mornings at the nursery; now she was there until six o'clock every day. But she still earned less than half of what Dad used to get.

At home, Dad was doing the cooking – if you could

call it that. Oven chips and fish fingers were about Dad's limit, with baked beans when he felt adventurous. I never knew you could get tired of chips, or fed up with sticky buns from the shop.

One night when Mum got in from work, totally exhausted, she found that Dad hadn't done any cooking at all. He came up from the basement, looking guilty. "Oh, sorry, love. I didn't notice the time, I was finishing that partition wall…"

Mum glared at him. I thought they were about to have another row – but no. She said nothing at all. In total silence she started getting a meal ready.

I almost asked her if she needed any help, but that would look as if I was taking her side against Dad. I wasn't on anybody's side, or rather I was on both. I mean, it wasn't Dad's fault that he was out of work, or Mum's fault that she was tired.

If Aladdin's genie had suddenly appeared and offered me one single wish, it wouldn't be to win the Lottery. It would be to have things back as they used to be – when we were happy. (Funny. We were happy and we hardly even noticed, until it stopped.)

Just then Grace came in with the local paper. We had stopped getting a daily paper, and we only got the *Westhaven Weekly* for the job adverts.

"Look what's in the paper," she said.

"Here is the news," I announced. "A lorry-load of glue has been spilt on the M25. Police are advising all vehicles to stick to their own lanes."

"Oh, shut up. What does 'marina' mean, Dad?"

"A place for boats to tie up. Pleasure boats, usually, not fishing boats. Why do you want to know?"

"It says here that they want to build a marina in

Westhaven – look."

"NEW MARINA – YES OR NO?" was the headline. Four whole pages were given over to the subject. (Because for Westhaven this was big, big news, like "PRIME MINISTER POISONED" would be for the *Times*.)

It looked quite good. There were architects' drawings and maps showing what could be done, and how many millions of pounds it would all cost. Part of the Basin would have to be dredged out to give a deepwater area close to the shore. The Basin, I ought to explain, is a huge tidal lake just north of the town. At low tide it's mostly mud; even at high tide the water is quite shallow. Every year, boats run aground and have to be towed off.

When the water was made deep enough, long pontoons – sort of floating quays – would be built out from the shore, with space for hundreds of boats to moor up. It would be a safe harbour even in stormy weather, because the Basin is almost cut off from the sea.

"Why do they need to do all this? We've got a harbour already," said Hannah.

"Not a very big one," said Dad. "It says here that the new marina would be four times bigger."

With the marina, far more boats would be able to visit Westhaven. To attract them, there would be a brand new Leisure Complex, a swimming-pool with water-slides, a waterfront bar, a floating restaurant…

"It looks amazing," Mum said. "But where are they going to put it all?"

"Look at the map. They want to knock down all those old empty warehouses in Basin Street," I said.

Dad said, "The Council wanted to do that years ago, but they never had the money. So where's the money for all this coming from?"

"Some company called Grandfield Enterprises."

"Never heard of them," said Dad suspiciously. "They can't be local, that's for sure."

Grandfield Enterprises, a London-based company, have developed two similar projects, one in Dorset, the other on the west coast of Scotland. Both have been very successful.

The paper showed photos to prove it. Rows of gleaming white yachts, neatly moored; laughing kids on a water-slide; elegant buildings reflected in the calm waters of the marina. "It all looks very posh," Mum said rather doubtfully.

"Bit too posh for Westhaven, you mean?" said Dad.

Several town councillors are in favour of the scheme. They believe it will add to Westhaven's existing attractions and bring in much-needed extra visitors. "Westhaven depends on the tourist trade," said Councillor Nigel Fitton, "and in the last few years it has declined noticeably. We must take action if our town is to survive." Councillor Joyce Brown said the marina would provide many new jobs.

"Oh!" said Grace. "You might get a job there, Dad. Helping to build the place, I mean."

"Don't get your hopes up," Dad said. "A thing like this takes ages to get going – years, probably. And I bet they won't use local workmen, anyway." But all the same, he looked less gloomy than he had been recently.

Mum smiled. "We can always hope."

"Hey, listen to this." I pretended to read from the

paper: "Four pedigree sheepdogs have gone missing. They have either been stolen or escaped from their kennels. The police say they have no leads."

And Dad laughed. He actually laughed.

Chapter 4

What do you get if you cross a cow with a seagull?

A pat on the head.

I soon found out that not everyone liked the marina project. One of our neighbours, Miss Grindlay, thought it was a dreadful idea. She was a member of the Westhaven Society, keen to preserve the history of the town.

"We don't approve. Of course we don't," she said to Mum. She had knocked on our door with a letter to the Town Council; she wanted Mum and Dad to sign it. "How can they even consider doing this? We shall fight them, have no fear. Fight them tooth and nail."

"But surely those old warehouses in Basin Street are not worth saving," said Mum. "They're almost falling down by themselves."

"Oh, it's not *those*. They're modern – early Fifties. They're of no great interest. It's what they'll be replaced with – a total eyesore! A concrete monstrosity, right on the edge of the oldest part of town! It will destroy the unique atmosphere of the harbour area."

"I suppose so," said Mum. She didn't sound convinced. "But don't you think the town needs something like this, to bring in more visitors?"

"In my opinion it's far more likely to drive people away. Leisure Centre! Water-slides!" She was almost spitting with disgust. "And moorings for those dreadful power boats! We certainly don't need more of those in Westhaven."

"What we do need more of, though, is jobs," said Mum. "I'm sorry. I can't sign your letter."

Miss Grindlay went off in a huff. "Oh dear," said Mum. "She'll probably never speak to me again."

"We can always hope," I said.

More seriously, though, Neddy was against the idea too. Neddy is a friend of ours. His real name is Edward, but only his grandmother calls him that. His parents got divorced ages ago, and he lives with his grandmother in Fountain Square.

Neddy, with his glasses and his untidy red hair, looks a bit like the mad scientists you see in films. He even owns a white lab coat. All that's missing is the Frankenstein monster on his laboratory table. (He does have a laboratory, but only for chemistry experiments. His grandmother doesn't mind the smell because she thinks it's educational.)

Neddy's extremely clever in almost every subject, except sport. But he is a bit odd sometimes. I used to feel rather nervous of him, because he was always taking the mick out of me for believing in God. He came along to the church Youth Club, but only so that he could laugh about it afterwards.

But lately he seemed to have stopped doing that – stopped laughing, I mean. He was still coming to the club every week, and really listening (unlike most other people) to Andy's talks.

When I mentioned this to Mum, she said, "Do you think he wants to become a Christian?"

"I don't know," I said. It was often hard to know what went on in Neddy's mind.

"You could always try asking him."

"I suppose so… but I don't want him to start laughing at me again."

"Well, don't say anything just yet," Mum said. "But pray about it. We'll both pray, shall we?"

So I prayed that Neddy would come to know God. But nothing had happened – not yet, anyway.

At the moment, his mind was focused on the marina project. He was just as angry as Miss Grindlay, but for different reasons.

"It will completely ruin the Basin," he said. "Do you know how many different birds breed there? At least twenty different species, and some are quite rare. The ringed plover, for instance, and the black-tailed godwit."

"So?" said Jake. "They'll still survive, won't they? I mean, the marina isn't going to take over the entire Basin, only the bit nearest the town."

"Oh sure. Once it's built, there will be maniacs in power boats zooming all over the place. No more peace and quiet. They'll pollute the water and scare all the wildlife – they'll turn the Basin into an enormous boating pond. It will never be the same."

"I don't see what's so wonderful about it now," I said. "It's just a huge mud-bank. Smelly, too."

Neddy said, "You'd think differently if you were a grey plover on your winter migration. The Basin is an important stopping-place for lots of migrants – there's nothing else like it for a hundred miles."

"Well, to me people are more important than birds," I said.

"What do you mean?" asked Neddy.

"I mean, if the marina goes ahead, my dad might get work."

"That's true. He might – for a year or two. But then, when it's all finished, he'd be out of work again… back to square one. And for that you'd destroy the Basin?"

I nodded.

"Absolutely criminal," said Neddy.

"That reminds me… what happened to the burglar who fell into wet cement? He became a hardened criminal."

This didn't seem to go down too well, so I tried another one. "What happened to the crook who stole a calendar?"

"He got twelve months," said Jake. "Which is what you ought to get, for cruelty."

"Cruelty?"

"Yes. Inflicting your painful jokes on innocent people who never did you any harm."

Neddy got up. "I can't take any more – I'm off. I want to have a look at the place where they plan to do the damage."

Jake and I decided to go too.

"All right," said Neddy. "On one condition – no more jokes."

Chapter 5

My dad got mad at me yesterday – he found my sister smoking.

So why did he get mad at you?

Because I was the one who set her on fire.

The sea is on the south side of town; the Basin is on the north. A wide channel connects them. The harbour opens off this channel, and all around it lies a maze of small, narrow streets. This is the oldest part of Westhaven. Tourists and film directors love it. There are antique shops, little tea-rooms, and shops selling T-shirts with rude messages on them. As usual on a summer Saturday, it was heaving with people.

But as we headed northwards, the streets grew quieter. Soon we were in Basin Street – a different world. On either side were high walls topped with barbed wire. Beyond them you could see the upper storeys of the old warehouses. The windows were boarded up, the gateways barred with corrugated iron.

"Who cares if they knock all this lot down?" said Jake.

"I expect Neddy does," I said. "It's an ideal habitat for rats – there's nowhere else like it for a hundred miles. Where will all the poor rats go if their homes are destroyed?"

"Shush," said Neddy.

"But that wasn't a joke," I protested. "I'm serious. Why should rats be less important than redshanks?"

"Oh do shut up for a minute. I thought I heard something – in there." He pointed towards the wall.

We listened, but there wasn't a sound. The whole length of Basin Street was empty. Nothing moved, except a few old bits of newspaper that twitched in the breeze.

"What did you hear?" Jake whispered.

"People talking. But quietly – like they didn't want to be overheard."

"They probably heard *us*," I said. "They could be listening to us right now."

It was a creepy thought. Were we being spied on through a crack in the boarded windows? Was anything alive in this dead-looking place?

After a while we went on. We came to a narrow alley leading off the street, with high walls on either side. At the far end of it was the gleam of sunlight on water.

"Must be the Basin," said Jake.

We went down to take a look. Stepping out from between the prison-like walls, we found ourselves on an open, breezy shore. The tide was in; small waves lapped gently on the pebbles. Blue water stretched far out beneath a huge empty sky.

"Hey, this is nice," I said. "I can just imagine sitting here at the waterfront café, sipping a drink, watching all the boats in the marina. I think they should start work tomorrow."

Neddy's face darkened. "Not if I can help it," he said.

"Where are all those birds that you're so keen on?" Jake said, and Neddy pointed out a few of them.

"You said there were hundreds," I complained.

"There are. Low tide is a much better time to see them, when they come to search for food in the mud."

I still thought the marina was worth more than a few seagulls. But what was the point in arguing? It was up to the Town Council to decide, not us. If they went ahead with it, there would be nothing Neddy could do.

We were going back up the narrow lane, when suddenly we all stopped dead. For we had heard someone scream.

There was the sound of running feet, and then the scream again. It came from over the wall which towered above us.

"Give me a leg-up," I said to Jake. But even standing on his shoulders, I couldn't reach the top of the wall. What was going on in there?

The noises changed. We heard laughter and voices shouting. Then there was the crash of breaking glass.

"Go on, Sam! Do it again!"

"Yeah, play it again, Sam!"

Tinkle, tinkle. More glass breaking.

"It's only kids," said Neddy, sounding relieved. "I wonder how they got in there?"

Just around the corner we noticed a doorway in the wall. Planks had been nailed across it, but there were gaps between them, especially at the bottom. Jake put his hand through and pushed the door. It creaked open; we peered through the gaps in the planks.

Between the door and the warehouse there was an

open yard, strewn with rubbish. Crates and cardboard boxes had been piled up in the middle, as if for a bonfire. At the far side, close to the warehouse itself, was a group of kids. Well, not kids – they looked older than us. I recognised Greg Wilder, a well-known trouble-maker from Year 10.

The gang seemed to be trying to get into the warehouse. There was a window at ground-floor level, with metal bars across it; Greg was reaching through the bars to pick bits of broken glass out of the window-frame.

"Who's going in?" he shouted. "We need someone skinny."

"I'll do it. I'm not scared," said a voice I knew.

I almost fell over with shock. It was Hannah – my sister.

What was she doing with that crowd? Then I noticed a friend of hers, Tanya Gordon. Tanya was going out with a boy called Ollie – yes, he was there too. Plus a couple of other Year 10 boys, whose names I didn't know.

If Dad saw them, he would have a fit. He didn't like Tanya much; he said she was a bad influence. (That was after he caught Tanya and Hannah smoking in our shed.) What would he say about this lot?

The wind caught the open door, and its hinges squeaked again. Tanya looked round suddenly and saw us.

"Look out! Spies!" she shouted.

Six hostile faces turned towards us. We didn't wait to see what they would do… we ran.

They would probably have caught us, but the planks across the doorway slowed them down. They could only wriggle through one at a time. We made it around the corner into Harbour Walk while they were still half-way down Basin Street. After that it was easy to get lost in the crowds.

"Phew!" said Jake. "Did you see the look on Greg's face? I'm going to keep out of his way from now on."

I only wished I could keep out of Hannah's way. She must have spotted me… But then I thought, that's stupid. What have I got to feel bad about? She's the one who should be feeling guilty.

"That wasn't your sister back there, was it?" said Neddy. He sounded as if he couldn't quite believe it.

"It might have been," I said. "Look, don't tell anyone else about it, okay? If it *was* Hannah, and Dad finds out, she'll be in deep, deep trouble."

"All right," said Jake. "But if Hannah's got mixed up with Greg and that lot, you'd better tell her to watch out. Bad news, they are."

Chapter 6

Doctor! Doctor! Promise me you'll cure my spots.

Sorry, I never make rash promises.

When Hannah got back, she went straight up to her room. I followed her.

These days she keeps her room locked. You have to knock at the door; usually she won't let you in, and if she does, you wish she hadn't. She's painted the walls and ceiling dark brown, and the curtains are always drawn. It feels like walking into a Stone Age cave, but instead of bones crunching under your feet, there are empty crisp packets, Coke cans, and forgotten school-books.

Mum has given up on Hannah's room. She says if Hannah wants to live in a pigsty, then let her. Maybe, one day, she'll get tired of the mess. (Yes, and one day, pigs may fly.)

When Hannah heard my voice, she opened the door at once, then locked it behind me. She looked very angry. Somehow she kept her voice to a whisper – a furious whisper.

"What were you doing, spying like that? Have you been following us?"

"Of course not," I said. "We never knew you were in there."

"Oh yeah? So what were you doing in Basin Street – playing hopscotch?"

"We wanted to see where they're going to build the marina, that's all. And then we heard somebody scream. We were just trying to find out what was going on. I mean it sounded like a murder or something."

"It was only Tanya," said Hannah. "Acting stupid as usual."

"Better make her keep the noise down if you don't want to be spied on. You're lucky we were the only ones that heard you."

"Oh." Her fury had died down a bit. "So you're not going to tell on me?"

I didn't answer that, because I hadn't decided yet. Would it be best to tell Mum and Dad, so that they could stop her getting into even worse trouble? *Could* they stop her, without locking her in the cellar? She was very strong-willed.

She said sullenly, "It's not as if we were doing anything wrong."

"Smashing windows isn't wrong? Breaking into a building is suddenly quite legal?"

"Oh, that. Nobody wants that old place. It's all going to be knocked down, so what's the problem if a few windows get broken?"

"Why did you want to get inside?" I asked. "To nick things?"

"There's nothing left that's worth nicking."

"Why, then?"

"I dunno. We were bored, I suppose. It was something to do."

I made up my mind. "Look, I won't tell Mum and Dad about it, as long as you promise something."

"And what do you want me to promise, little brother?"

"To stop going around with Greg and that lot. Jake says they're bad news."

"Huh! What does Jake know about anything? He's just a stupid kid, and so are you." She was getting mad again. "It's none of your business, anyway. I don't criticise *your* friends, do I?"

I said, "It is my business. I don't want to see you getting into trouble."

"Oh, really?"

I shook my head.

"In that case you won't tell Dad, then. You'll forget you ever saw me today." Suddenly she grabbed me by the shoulders. "But it wasn't true what you just said. You *do* like to see me getting into trouble. Big bad Hannah, not like good little Ben, who always does exactly what he's told... you love it. Don't you?"

I felt my face go red (not that she would notice in the cave-like gloom). Certainly, when I was younger, I did enjoy seeing Hannah get told off. It made up for the fact that she was bigger and older and cleverer than me. I used to try to be extra well-behaved on the days when Hannah was naughty.

"Maybe I used to," I said, "but not any more."

"Oh, you make me sick." She pushed me away from her. "You're such a little creep. Scared to do anything at all in case Mum and Dad don't like it. Or God doesn't like it. Well, I've got news for you – there is no God, so why bother? You may as well do what you like."

It wasn't the first time I'd heard her say that – about there being no God. (She kept telling Dad she wanted to stop going to church, and Dad said, "No church – no pocket money.")

"You're wrong," I said. "There is a God, whether you believe in him or not."

She laughed. "Yes, that's what you've been brought up to think. You've been brainwashed into it. Just because Mum and Dad believe in God, you believe too. You should try thinking things out for yourself, not swallowing whatever they tell you. They don't know everything, do they?"

"They know a lot more than you do," I said.

"No they don't. They believe whatever the minister tells them. And the minister says whatever the church tells him to say. And it's all a load of total rubbish!"

"Fine," I said, "if that's what you think. But why are you getting so angry about it?"

"I'm angry because you think you're better than me. *You* want to tell *me* what to do! Well, listen to this. I'll go on seeing my friends if I want to. And if you go running to Mum and Dad, telling tales, then I'll tell them how you used to nick money out of Mum's purse."

"That was ages ago," I protested. "I was only about seven."

"Oh, so you've stopped doing it, have you? They won't believe that, though, if any more money goes missing. And I can make sure that it does."

I stared at her. She wouldn't – surely she wouldn't.

"I think that's only fair," she said, grinning. "If you get me in trouble, then I'll get you in trouble. Okay? Is it a deal?"

I told Jake and Neddy what she had said. "And I was only trying to help…"

"Boy, am I glad I don't have a sister," said Jake.

"She hasn't always been as bad as this," I said. "She used to be okay. But now she just seems to hate everybody. She hates the entire family, apart from Tubs and Jerry. She doesn't like school, she loathes church, and she thinks Westhaven is the most boring place on the entire planet."

"I think that's what they call adolescence," said Neddy. "It will probably happen to us one day, too."

"It's not going to happen to me – not like that. I won't let it," I said.

Neddy said, "That's like saying you won't let yourself catch measles."

"It *could* be measles that Hannah's got," I said. "She's quite spotty enough. On the other hand, measles doesn't affect the brain, does it? Perhaps she's got rabies."

"It can't be rabies. She isn't foaming at the mouth."

"You wouldn't say that if you'd seen her earlier."

But it was time for a change of subject. Illness… doctors… now which of my vast collection of Doctor jokes should I tell?

"Doctor! Doctor! I keep thinking I'm a pair of curtains!"

But Jake had heard it before. He said wearily, "You ought to pull yourself together."

"What a double-act you two could be," said Neddy. "The greatest thing since…"

"Laurel and Hardy?" I said hopefully. "Morecambe and Wise?"

"Bread and cheese, I was going to say."

"There's nothing funny about bread and cheese."

"That's what I mean," said Neddy.

Chapter 7

Doctor! Doctor! I just crashed through a window!

So where's the pain?

It was the start of the summer holidays. Great! Well, actually, not so great. Not this year.

We wouldn't be going out much – at least not to anywhere that cost money. We couldn't even look forward to going away. Mum said we *might* go camping for a few days in August, but she wasn't making any promises.

Normally, Mum would be at home all day in the holidays. But now that she was working full-time, she couldn't take all those weeks off – and anyway, we needed the money. So instead of Mum at home and Dad at work, it was the other way round.

Dad was still spending a lot of time on the basement. It was starting to look like a proper flat: two good-sized rooms, plus kitchen and bathroom, and a front door with steps up to the street. Grace and I helped him as much as we could. I did some painting, Grace made sandwiches and endless cups of tea.

Hannah wasn't around much. She had got herself a

summer job in a shop on the sea front. It sold ice creams, toy boats, plastic spades, beach mats… all the things that Piggies need to make their holiday complete. (Plus postcards showing total darkness, with the title *Westhaven By Night*. Hannah stuck one of those on her bedroom door.)

When Mum asked if she liked the job, she said, "Not much. The money's okay but it's boring. The only excitement we get is when some kid tries to nick something."

"Can I come and buy something in your shop?" asked Grace.

"If you like. But don't expect a free ice-cream – the boss watches us like a hawk. Mum, I'm off round Tanya's. See you later."

Most evenings she went round Tanya's, or at least that's where she said she was going. I wondered if Tanya told *her* mum that she was going to see Hannah. But who cared? If they wanted to get into trouble, then let them. It was none of my business.

Each time Dad went down to the Job Centre, he came back looking depressed.

"There's nothing at all," he said, "or nothing that I'm any good at. Plenty of jobs for qualified chefs and hotel receptionists and so on."

"You could try being a hotel chef, Dad," I said. "And tonight's choice of menu is: fish fingers, fish fingers, fish fingers, or beans on toast."

"Of course, things may be different in the wintertime," Dad said, trying to cheer himself up. "If hotels want any building work done, they do it in winter, when they're quiet. But that's months away."

"Never mind," said Grace, sounding exactly like Mum. "Have a cup of tea."

"Thanks, love."

"Dad, you *will* get something soon," she said. "I just know you will. I've been praying about it – so don't worry."

Dad's eyes met mine, and I saw what he was thinking: "I hope she's right, but I can't quite believe it."

This came as a shock to me. Grace, who was only nine, had more faith in God than Dad had! Grace was quite certain her prayers would be answered. Dad wasn't nearly so sure – and neither was I.

"Grace," Dad said rather hesitantly, "you know, don't you, that God doesn't always give us everything we ask for."

"I know *that*," she said. "But last night, when I was praying, I sort of felt God was telling me something… to stop worrying, because it was all going to be okay. And something about hands…"

That reminded me of what Andy had said weeks ago. "Our times are in God's hands?"

"Yes! That was it. So we don't need to worry."

I looked at her rather enviously. After all, I had been praying too, every day. But God hadn't spoken to *me* like that. Or maybe Grace had imagined it?

Grace takes after Mum – always looking on the bright side. Dad and I are more cautious. "I'll believe it when I see it," is one of Dad's sayings, the opposite to Mum's favourite, "There's always hope."

Mum will talk to anybody about anything, but Dad is much quieter. And he doesn't like the whole world knowing our problems. He really hated it when people at church kept asking if he'd found a new job yet. He would answer them politely, but I could tell he was fuming inside.

One Sunday Dad announced that he wasn't going to church. He wanted to finish sanding the floors in the basement, he said.

Grace stared at him. "But Dad! What's the matter? You always go to church."

"Well, then, it won't hurt to miss one Sunday, will it?" he said.

"That's so unfair!" cried Hannah. "I've been saying that for years, but you never let *me* miss any! Well if Dad's not going, I'm not going." And she was off out the door before anyone could stop her.

Mum looked as if there were things she wanted to say. But Dad had disappeared into the basement. Soon we heard the noise of the sanding machine, as harsh as a dentist's drill.

"Mum," said Grace, "are you still coming to church?"

"Of course I am. Now get ready, if you're coming."

We sat in our usual place at church. It felt odd with just the three of us. A couple of people came up to us to ask if Dad was all right.

"He's fine," Mum said cheerfully. "He just wanted to finish some work around the house."

"Oh. No news on the job situation, then?"

"No, nothing yet."

When they'd moved on, I whispered, "Why do people have to be so nosey?"

"Oh, Ben. You're just like your dad. They're not being nosey – they care about us."

"Okay, but why can't they care about us without asking nosey questions?"

"Shhh."

The service began. I felt as if it was all happening a long way off. Bright, happy songs about praising God had nothing to do with the way I was feeling. Grace gave me a funny look when she saw I wasn't singing.

"What's the matter?"

"I've got a sore throat," I muttered. This wasn't exactly a lie. I did have a pain inside me, but not in my throat. It went deeper than that.

Doctor! Doctor! I keep thinking I'm –

Oh, shut up.

Chapter 8

If every car in Britain was painted red, what would happen?

Britain would become a red carnation.

"Isn't this your friend Neddy?" said Dad.

"What? In the paper? Show me."

It *was* Neddy. The photo showed him holding one end of a banner which said, *S.O.S. – Save Our Seabirds.* Loads of other people were there too. I recognised Miss Grindlay and the Biology teacher from school. They were on the steps of the Town Hall, protesting against the marina. Bird-watchers and nature-lovers had joined with people from the Westhaven Society, all saying No to the marina scheme.

The letters page of the *Weekly* was full of the subject. There were 6 letters for it and 6 against. ("That's because the editor doesn't want to upset anyone," said Dad. "He needs all the readers he can get.")

"The marina will bring new life to Westhaven – and we need it."

"This badly-planned scheme will be the death of Westhaven's tourist trade."

"The glorious, unspoiled Basin should be made into a nature reserve."

"The Basin is ugly and smelly, a disgrace to the town."

"We love the marina scheme! Start work at once!"

"We hate it. Ban it for ever."

Because of helping Dad, I hadn't seen much of Neddy in the last few days. When I called round, I found he was busy making another banner. He was cutting out the letters and his grandmother was stitching them.

Neddy's grandmother, Mrs Fortescue, is quite a scary person. Until she retired a few years ago, she was a school head – and she still acts like one. She's very strict on good behaviour, politeness and keeping the rules.

So I was surprised to see her making a banner which said, SAVE THE BASIN! COUNCIL OUT, OUT, OUT!

"Well? What do you think of our latest creation?" she said, holding it up.

"Er… very eye-catching," I said.

Neddy said, "We shouldn't be letting you see it, Ben. After all, you're on the side of the enemy."

His grandmother fixed me with her eyes, which were as sharp as the needle she was using. (Like Neddy, she wears glasses, but she doesn't miss much.) "Surely, Benjamin, you're not in favour of that appalling scheme?" she said.

"Well, yes. I am actually. But only because it might help my dad to find work."

"That's rather like saying it was a good idea to build the *Titanic*. After all it gave the shipbuilders some work to do."

She was just like Neddy. They could both say clever

things that I had no answer to. (Except of course by telling a joke. *Heard about the ship that sank with its cargo of yo-yos? It went down 17 times*. But somehow, I could tell that wouldn't go down too well with Mrs Fortescue.)

"What's the banner for?" I asked. "Are you going to attack the Town Hall?"

"Not telling," said Neddy. "As I said – you're the enemy."

"Oh, don't be daft. Do you think I'm spying for the Council? If I was a spy, I ought to pretend to be on your side."

"Good thinking, young man," said Mrs Fortescue. "Edward, there's no need to be *quite* so secretive. Everyone will know about our next demonstration soon enough. In fact, the more people who know, the better. It won't be much of a protest march if no one turns up!"

"Are you going to march right through the town?" I asked.

"That's right," said Neddy. "And if the Council still won't listen, then we're planning –"

"Edward!" said his grandmother in her head teacher voice. "Remember, we agreed not to talk about that. Not to *anyone*."

"Yes. Of course. Stupid of me," said Neddy.

She said, "Why don't you two go out and get some exercise? It's the holidays. You ought to be getting some fresh air into your lungs. Go and play football, or something."

It was an order. We went out.

"Neddy," I said, "what's the big secret? What are you planning to do?"

"My lips are sealed," he said. "You'll find out one day. Hey, look at that car. Not bad, eh?"

It was a red Ferrari, parked outside Sea View. Just then a man came out of the hotel. He was smartly dressed in a business suit and tie – not at all like a normal Piggy. (Or not the kind of Piggy that stays at Sea View. This one was more the Grand Hotel type.)

I said, "Bet you he owns that car. Sea View must be going up in the world."

But the man didn't get into the car. Instead, he walked briskly across the Square and rang our doorbell.

"What on earth does he want?" I wondered aloud.

"Not being psychic," said Neddy, "I can't answer that. Why not go and find out?"

Dad answered the door. He looked annoyed at being disturbed while he was working. But by the time we got closer, he was looking rather pleased. Had we won a small prize in the Lottery? (Not too likely, since we hadn't bought a ticket.)

"It's nearly ready," Dad was saying. "A few more days and you could move in. Would you like to see it?"

He led the stranger down the outside steps and into the basement. I wondered what the well-dressed man would think of it, with paint pots everywhere, and bare wooden floors, and no furniture. Through the front window I saw Grace scurrying round, collecting dirty coffee mugs.

After quite some time, Dad and the stranger came out again. They were both smiling.

"I'm glad to have found a place at last," the man said. "I was beginning to think I would have to sleep under the pier."

Dad said, "It's the holiday season. From now till September, you'd have trouble finding an empty broom cupboard, never mind a flat. By the way, how did you hear about this place?"

"A boy mentioned you at the hotel over there."

Good old Jake, I thought. I must remember to thank him.

"Must dash," the man said. "Got to get back to town tonight." He strode back across the Square, got into the red Ferrari (so it *was* his), and roared away. Maybe, if he was going to live in our house, he would give me a ride in it sometime…

Dad took a cheque out of his pocket and looked at it lovingly. "Five hundred quid deposit, and a month's rent in advance," he said.

"He must be rolling in money," I said. "Did you see that car? A red Ferrari – my dream car."

"Dream on," said Dad. "Meanwhile we've got work to do. He wants to move in as soon as possible; I said we could be ready in three days. Think we can do it?"

Chapter 9

This is an announcement for passengers travelling to London Euston.

The train now approaching platforms 2,3,4,5,6 and 7 is coming in sideways.

We did it. The flat was ready in three days, and furnished, more or less. The furniture came from our own house, or was bought second-hand; probably none of it would impress the Ferrari man. But at least it made the rooms look less bare.

"Not bad," said Dad. "I wouldn't mind living here myself."

"You can't afford it," said Mum, laughing. "I still can't believe how much rent that man is prepared to pay. I mean, it's as much as we could get from a whole family on holiday."

Dad said, "And the best part is, he'll probably stay on here long after the holiday-makers have gone home. The company he works for has sent him to Westhaven for at least six months, maybe longer."

"If he can afford a car like that," said Grace, "why doesn't he have a house of his own?"

"If I had a car like that, I'd live in it all the time," I said.

Dad laughed. "He does have a house of his own, but it's in London. He doesn't want to sell it. He's planning to go back there most weekends. But he will be around during the week – so listen, you lot. Just behave yourselves. Remember we've got somebody else living in our house now."

That was rather a strange thought. I'm not like Jake, who was brought up in a hotel. To him, having strangers around all the time is part of normal life. But to me, it felt as if we were being invaded.

Mum said, "Wasn't it lucky that he found his way to our door?"

"I don't think it was lucky," said Grace, and everyone stared at her. "What I mean is, it wasn't just luck. It's like in my dream – God's looking after us."

Mum and Dad nodded in agreement. They both looked very happy today. (It's amazing what a big fat cheque can do for people.)

But Hannah looked annoyed. "That's stupid," she said. "Whenever anything good happens, you say it's God looking after us. But what about the bad things? God must have caused them too. If you believe in him, that is."

Mum said, "God doesn't *cause* bad things –"

Hannah interrupted her. "Thank you God for Dad being out of work. Thank you God for homeless people. Thank you God for the famine in Africa. Thank you for looking after us all!"

"That's enough, Hannah," said Dad sharply.

"Why can't you see how stupid it is?" cried Hannah. "There is no God. There's no one there looking after us. Little kids can believe in God if they like, but grown-ups ought to have more sense." And she stamped out of the room. When she slammed the door, the whole house seemed to tremble.

Dad looked as if he was going to go after her, but Mum stopped him. "It's no good. When she's in a mood like this, she just won't listen."

"Never mind, Mum," said Grace. "Maybe she'll grow out of it one day."

Grandad rang up to see if we could do a bit of shopping for him. Usually he did his own shopping, while a neighbour kept an eye on Granny – he couldn't leave her on her own. But the neighbours were away on holiday.

I said I would go. Now that the flat was finished, I was feeling bored. (And so was Dad – he had started working ferociously on the garden.)

I took the dog with me, which was a bad move. He doesn't like being tied up outside shops, and then when we got back to Grandad's place, he wouldn't go into the lift. I had to struggle up three flights of stairs carrying the shopping, with Jerry pulling at the lead.

Granny used to be fond of Jerry. But today, when she saw him, she gave a little scream and cowered away.

"It's all right, Granny, he's quite friendly. Don't you remember him?"

"Take it away! Take it away!" cried Granny. She wouldn't be quiet until we had shut Jerry in the bedroom, out of sight.

Grandad gave me a drink and a Mars Bar. He wanted to hear all our news. I told him about Mr Lewis, the Ferrari man, who had moved in two days before.

"What's he like, this chap?" asked Grandad.

"I'd say he's a bit younger than Dad. Tall, fair-haired, very smart clothes. Hannah thinks he's good-looking. Dad told her to keep off him, he's old enough to be her father."

Grandad laughed. "I meant, is he nice? A friendly type?"

"Not friendly, exactly. He's polite enough, but he keeps himself to himself. We've hardly seen him. He goes out early and comes back late. You'd hardly know he was there."

Granny was not listening. As usual, she was gazing out of the window. The flat had a nice view over the park; beyond the treetops you could catch a glimpse of the sea. (Not as nice as the view from their old house on the cliff-top, though. Did Grandad miss the old place? He never talked about it.)

Granny pushed me aside quite roughly – I was blocking her view. I went to look out of the side window, but there the outlook was not so pretty. A fire-escape, a row of garages, and a wooden fence surrounding a bit of waste ground.

"What are they going to build over there, Grandad?" I asked, wondering if there would be a job for Dad in it.

"They *were* going to put up some holiday flats, but the company ran out of money. Goodness knows if it will ever get built now. The local children treat the place like an adventure playground."

There were some kids in there now, building a den out of boxes and bits of junk. Then a gang of older kids arrived and chased the little ones off. They looked like… yes, I was pretty sure they were Greg Wilder and his mates.

Was Hannah there too? I couldn't see her. Then I remembered she would be at the shop all afternoon – which was just as well. She was quite mad enough to do something crazy right under the windows of Grandad's flat.

One of the big boys started knocking down the little kids' den, but Greg stopped him. He got something out of his pocket and held it out. After a minute I saw what he was doing. He had a cigarette lighter; he was trying to set fire to the den.

It didn't catch alight to begin with, so the gang collected odd bits of rubbish and added them to the pile. Soon it was blazing away. Greg stood admiring it, while his friends threw on more boxes and bits of wood.

"What's going on out there?" asked Grandad.

"Only some kids having a bonfire."

"What? Look at the way the wind's blowing. If they're not careful, they'll have the whole fence alight!"

He pointed to the wooden fence that surrounded the building site. I saw that if it caught fire, the row of garages would be next. But the gang didn't seem to care. They danced around the flames, yelling and whooping like the lost tribes of the Amazon.

Grandad rang for the fire brigade. Three minutes later we heard the siren; the gang heard it too. They ran off in the opposite direction – all except for Greg. He went away slowly, turning his head to look back at the fire, as if he could hardly bear to leave it.

The firemen put the flames out very quickly. Soon there was nothing left except a steaming black heap and a smoky smell.

"Did you see the way that youngster looked at the fire?" said Grandad. "I wouldn't be at all surprised if he turned out to be an arsonist."

"A what?"

"Someone who starts fires on purpose. Very dangerous – don't you ever try it. There now, Winnie, it's all over. Nothing to worry about."

But Granny hadn't even noticed what was happening. She was still in her seat by the front window, gazing out at the park.

"Oh la la la oh la la," she sang to herself. "Oh la la la oh la la."

Grandad sighed. "She does that for hours on end sometimes."

"Does it get on your nerves?" I said.

"It does. Still, at least she's happy. And how's that sister of yours? I haven't seen her for a while."

"Hannah, you mean? She's…" I stopped because I wasn't sure what to say. I didn't want to get Hannah into trouble, and yet I desperately wanted to talk to someone.

"What's the matter?" said Grandad.

"Grandad, if I tell you something, you won't tell Mum, will you? Promise?" I told him about the bad crowd of friends Hannah went around with, and the threats she had made if I told on her. And about her terrible moods, hating all of us, hating church, hating God.

"Poor Hannah," Grandad said. "She doesn't sound at all happy."

"That's the understatement of the year. Mum keeps saying she'll grow out of it, but she's getting worse, not better. What can we do?"

"The best thing you can do," said Grandad, "is pray for her. Every time she gets in a mood, don't get angry back at her – just pray. I don't mean out loud! And I'll pray too. I get plenty of time for that, these days."

"Oh la la la oh la la," Granny sang. "Little ones to him belong, we are weak but he is strong. Oh la la la…"

"That sounded like part of a hymn," I said.

"You're right. *Jesus loves me, this I know…* She's forgotten a lot of other things, but sometimes she still remembers that."

"Grandad, do you pray for Granny?"

He nodded.

"But she's not getting any better."

"No. She will be better one day – in heaven. In the place where there's no more sorrow, or crying, or pain. But I don't think she'll ever get better here on earth. I've stopped asking for that."

Granny didn't like us talking while she sang. Her voice was getting louder. "Oh la la la oh la la. Silence please, silence please. Oh la la la oh la la."

I whispered, "Grandad, why does God let bad things happen? Like Granny getting ill, and Dad losing his job? If God really loves us, why do bad things happen?"

"Well, now. That's a hard question. You know, don't you, that when God made the world, it was all good? But it got spoiled. People didn't want to keep God's rules. They wanted to go their own way – and so all kinds of bad things came into the world. Hatred, greed, violence… illness and pain… And ever since, there's been a war going on. A fight between good and evil."

"Is good going to win in the end?"

"The Bible says so. At the end, there'll be one great battle, and evil will be driven out for ever. But in the meantime, we've still got a fight on our hands."

"I don't understand," I said. "How can you fight against Granny's illness? You're not a doctor."

"What I have to fight against is inside me. Feeling angry with her, getting impatient, almost hating her – that's the evil I have to fight against. Do you see? I don't always win, mind. There are days when it's a losing battle."

"And what about Dad being out of work?"

"Ah, that's a different fight. You have different enemies – worrying too much, that's one. And forgetting to trust in God."

Or getting angry with God (like Hannah). Or angry with other people (like Dad). I was beginning to understand.

Grandad said, "You do worry quite a bit, don't you, son?"

I nodded. "Sometimes I lie awake for hours at night, thinking about what could happen. You know – what if we have to sell the house? What if Dad gets a job in London or somewhere? What if Mum and Dad start arguing again? What if Hannah gets in trouble with the police?"

"Does worrying do any good? Does it help the situation?"

"No, but… I just can't stop doing it."

"What you have to do," said Grandad, "is pray about the things that worry you. Put them in God's hands. And then leave them there! Don't keep taking them back in your own hands. The Bible says, *Leave*

all your worries with him, because he cares for you.
Here, let me write it down so you'll remember."

"Oh la la la. Cup of tea. Cup of tea, a cup of tea," Granny sang.

Grandad got up to put the kettle on.

"I'd better be getting back," I said. "Thanks, Grandad."

Chapter 10

Here is the News:

A large hole has suddenly appeared in the middle of Oxford Street.

The police are looking into it.

Andy, the Youth Minister, rang up to see if I wanted to go on the Friday Club camp. It was only three days away, but two sisters had dropped out at the last minute.

"It's all paid for," he said. "You wouldn't have to worry about that." (He knew I really wanted to go, but hadn't put my name down earlier because of the cost.) "And if you can think of anyone else who'd like to come, let me know."

I asked Dad if I could go. When I said it was all paid for, he looked suspicious. "We can pay," he said stiffly. "We don't need charity."

"It's free because someone else dropped out," I said. "Not because they think we can't afford it. Oh, please can I go, Dad? Please?"

"We'll see what your mum says," he muttered – so I knew it would be all right.

Who else should I invite – Jake or Neddy? Jake was my best friend, and he did come to Friday Club now and then... not as often as Neddy, though. I somehow had the feeling it would be better to ask Neddy.

I went round to see him.

"I *might* go," he said cautiously. "When is it? We've got that protest march on Saturday – I'm not missing that."

"You won't have to miss it. We don't leave until Sunday night. Oh, come on, Neddy – it'll be a good laugh. Last year nobody got to sleep until about two in the morning."

Neddy looked alarmed. "Don't let Grandmother hear that."

"Edward!" His grandmother called from the hall. "Be ready in five minutes, please."

"Where are you going?" I asked him.

"Out," he said.

"Yes, but where to?"

"That's none of your –" he started to say, then changed his mind. "Shopping. We're going shopping. I need some new shoes."

"What fun," I said. "See you later."

I hurried over to Sea View, where I found Jake gloomily vacuuming the lounge.

"Don't you think Neddy's been a bit strange lately?" I said. "Kind of secretive?"

Jake nodded. "I think it's all to do with the marina project, but he won't say."

"And now," I said, "he and his grandmother are setting out on some kind of secret mission. I'm going to follow them. Want to come?"

"Okay. Just let me put the Hoover away."

I kept watch from the window. By the time Jake came back, I had seen Neddy and Mrs Fortescue leave their house and go round the corner into Pump Street. We followed them, keeping well back, and dodging behind parked cars whenever we could. We got some funny looks from passers-by.

Once, I thought Neddy had seen us when he stopped to cross the street. But I wasn't sure. He and Mrs Fortescue walked slowly into the shopping centre. A boy and an old lady – they didn't *look* like people with a hidden purpose. But then why had Neddy lied to me?

Perhaps I'd been completely wrong. Because they were now going into a shoe shop.

"He was telling the truth after all," I said, disappointed. "The secret mission is just to buy shoes. Let's go home."

"No, wait a minute. It might be a trick…"

We ducked into a shop doorway, where we could keep an eye on the shoe shop entrance. As we waited, Jake suddenly nudged me.

"Look, it's your Ferrari man. In that shop over there."

Opposite us was a shop which had been empty for months. But now it was being opened up. Workmen carried furniture in from a van, and in the shop window Mr Lewis was fixing up a huge poster: OPENING SOON – WESTHAVEN MARINA EXHIBITION.

"Does he work for that company, then?" asked Jake. "The marina people?"

"Looks like it," I said. "Don't tell Neddy, though. He might arrange for thousands of seagulls to dive-bomb the Ferrari."

Interesting. If Mr Lewis did work for Grandfield, would he put in a good word for Dad when the building work started? I decided to be extra polite whenever I saw him.

Jake said, "Talking of Neddy, where is he? They've had enough time to buy seventeen pairs of shoes."

We walked casually past the shoe shop and glanced in. Strange – I couldn't see Neddy, or his grandmother. But then I realised that the shop had another exit at the back, leading out into Rupert Street. They must have gone out that way, probably as soon as they went in. They had given us the slip.

"How come this never happens in films?" said Jake bitterly. "James Bond never loses whoever he's following. Over roof-tops, through sewers, down lift shafts … and we can't even do it right in the High Street."

That reminded me. "What's the name of James Bond's goldfish?"

"James Pond, I suppose. Ha ha."

"Wrong again. It's Bubble-oh-seven."

Jake wasn't listening. "Know where we are?" he said. "Only about five minutes from Basin Street. I wonder if that's where they were heading?"

"We could take a look," I said. "But what if Greg and that lot are round there?"

"If they are, we'll hear them before they hear us," said Jake.

Basin Street was deserted, just like before. We went cautiously down it. The only sounds were the cries of seagulls. I could smell the smell of the Basin – seaweed, salt and mud.

When we came to the small doorway in the wall, Jake opened it gently. The yard inside was quiet and empty.

"You coming in?" said Jake.

I hesitated.

"Go on," he said. "What are you scared of?"

"I don't know. Isn't it against the law?"

"Breaking and entering – that's illegal," he said. "But we're not breaking in, are we? We're not going to do any damage, just explore a bit."

"Oh, well," I said. "Into the unknown." I squeezed through the gap in the planks.

There wasn't much to see in the yard. Where there had been a pile of boxes, all that remained was a mound of soft grey ash. It looked as if Greg and his mates had had another bonfire.

I wondered if the gang had tried again to get into the warehouse. The broken window was still broken. Had Hannah really wanted to climb through the bars? It didn't look possible, even for someone as skinny as she was. (What would have happened if she'd got stuck? I bet her so-called friends would have run off and left her there, struggling and shouting.)

"Hey, look at this!" said Jake softly.

He was standing by the main entrance to the building, a huge double door. I saw that it was open slightly. Jake heaved, and it groaned open further, heavy and slow like the door of a dungeon.

"Talk about stupid! They didn't need to break a window. They could have got in this way."

"They're not *that* stupid," I said uneasily. "Maybe the door wasn't open before."

"So who opened it?"

"I dunno. If Hannah or somebody did get in through that window, she might have unbolted the door from the inside."

Jake stepped through the doorway, into the darkness. He's quite brave when it comes to things like that – or else he's got no imagination. To me, it felt like that moment in a computer game, when you know you have to be ready. There are enemies in there, waiting to get you. Finger on the button… you have to kill them before they kill you…

But this was no game. This was real.

"Come *on*, Ben!" Jake called impatiently. "It's all right. There's no one here."

I took a deep breath and went in.

Chapter 11

Why was Cinderella no good at football?

Because she ran away from the ball.

Inside, the warehouse was vast. It was like a cathedral, filled with silence and a dim grey light. Long aisles of dusty shelves – all empty – stretched away into the distance.

Years ago, this place must have been full of activity. Fork-lift trucks fetching and carrying; lorries arriving in the yard; sacks and crates coming in by sea and leaving by road. Grandad says Westhaven was once quite a busy port. But that was in the days of small cargo boats. Nowadays it's all container ships and huge oil tankers, far too big for Westhaven harbour.

We wandered the length of the enormous room. Nothing moved, not even a scurrying mouse – but then I suppose the mice had eaten anything that was edible a long time ago. The warehouse had been empty for years and years.

At the end of the room there was a huge lift, big enough for a fork-lift truck. Jake pressed the button, but of course there was no reaction. The electricity had been turned off.

"If there's a lift," Jake whispered, "there must be another level."

"It *is* like a computer game," I muttered. "Why are we whispering, by the way?"

"I don't know." Suddenly Jake let out an ear-splitting yell. It echoed horribly in the emptiness.

"I wish you hadn't done that," I said. He looked as if he felt the same. In a room this size, even though it *seemed* empty, you couldn't be sure…

Jake opened a door near the lift, and found some stairs leading upwards. A bit more light came in here through a gap in the boarded-up window; without that, I don't think either of us would have dared to go up.

"Go on, then," I said. "You can't really say you've tried a game if you've only completed Level One."

On the floor above there was a wide corridor, almost in darkness. Doors opened off it on either side. Some led to offices, some to smaller storerooms, from what we could see in the narrow shafts of light that came in. Everywhere there was silence and a thick layer of dust.

I opened another door – and leapt backwards. There was an explosion of rushing wings, bright sunlight and cold air.

"It's all right," said Jake. "Only birds. Boy, Neddy ought to see this place."

Looking in, I saw another huge room, almost as big as the one downstairs. My eyes, adjusted for darkness, slowly got used to the light coming in from the windows in the roof. A lot of the glass was broken. Dozens of pigeons were flapping around; the floor was thick with bird-droppings.

I said, "They must have been living here for years."

"Yeah. It's a pigeon hotel – Sea View II."

"I bet you're glad you don't have to vacuum *that*

floor," I said.

"Sea View II," Jake said grandly, "is magnificently situated close to all of Westhaven's major attractions. Just a short flight from the Town Hall roof and the statues on the sea front. Eat out around the dustbins of Westhaven's many restaurants, or picnic in the park. Nestlings welcome. A shower in every room – weather permitting."

"Pigeon English spoken," I added.

The pigeons did not seem impressed. We got the feeling they would rather we left.

"Shut the door, or else they'll invade the whole place," said Jake.

"Who cares? It's all going to be knocked down anyway," I said, sounding like my sister.

We went back along the corridor. The stairs still led upwards, so we followed them. At the top was a door which opened onto the flat roof of the building.

"Do you think it's safe to go out there?" I said.

Jake said, "This part looks okay. But don't go and step on any windows, unless you want to visit the pigeons again."

Out on the roof, we had a wonderful view. The town lay spread out to the south of us, with the sea beyond it. Westward lay the harbour, full of brightly painted fishing boats and gleaming yachts. To the north was the Basin. The tide was out, so it was empty, apart from where the river looped between the mud-banks. Flocks of birds were sprinkled over the mud like white sugar on a dark brown cake.

The only blot on the landscape was Basin Street – the warehouse we stood on, and others like it. With their stained brickwork, their boarded windows and rusty barbed wire, they looked horrible, like something that died long ago and was never buried.

"No wonder they want to knock this lot down and rebuild," said Jake. "They ought to have done it years ago."

"Dad says the Council never had the money," I said.

"That won't be a problem for the Grandfield people," said Jake. "Not if they're all like Ferrari Man. Look, you can see the roof of our school."

"Jake, it's the summer holidays. Don't even mention the word school…" I stopped talking, because I'd just noticed something rather odd. It was a sunny day, but not exactly warm; a brisk east wind was blowing. And yet I could see a sort of shimmer in the air, like you get in very hot weather. In very hot weather or… above a bonfire?

It was over the roof of the farthest warehouse, right along Basin Street. As I stared at it, I saw a thin grey cloud of smoke, pale in the sunlight, like a layer of dirt on a window.

"Jake! I think that building's on fire! Look. Look."

Second by second the smoke grew thicker. This wasn't a bonfire in the yard; the smoke was rising from the roof and swirling out of the gaps in the windows.

"We'd better call the fire brigade," I said.

"Why?" said Jake. "You said yourself, it's going to be knocked down. Let it burn! There's nothing like a good fire."

"You're as bad as Greg," I said. "How do you know the fire won't spread? I'm going to ring 999."

I hurried down the long flights of stairs and through the empty building. Jake was close behind me. As I struggled through the planks across the doorway, I heard running feet in the street outside. The runner almost cannoned into me.

"Neddy!" I cried out. "What are you doing here?"

"Can't stop. Fire! Back there," he gasped.

"Yes, we know. Where's the nearest phone box?"

"Harbour Walk, I think," said Jake. "Come on."

Jake got there first, which annoyed me. I wanted to be the one who rang 999. Grandad hadn't let me do it, and now I had missed my chance again.

The fire brigade were not quite so quick off the mark this time – four and a half minutes. Attracted by the sirens and the rising cloud of smoke, a small crowd gathered in Basin Street. I wondered if Greg, the fire-lover, would appear.

The building was well ablaze by now. Flames leapt at the windows; we heard a great crash as part of the roof fell in. The firemen had hacked their way through the blocked-up gateway so that their engines could get into the yard. Now they were hosing water onto the building.

"They ought to be able to put it out fairly quickly," said Neddy. "An empty building – there's nothing that would burn in there, apart from the floors and the roof."

"How do you know?" said Jake. "Been inside, have you?"

Neddy looked startled for a minute. "Just an educated guess," he said.

"Come on, admit it," I said. "You've been in there."

"No."

Jake said, "Don't worry – we won't tell. We've gone in too. Well, not this one, but I suppose they're all alike."

"Keep your voice down!" Neddy whispered fiercely. "Do you want people to think you started the fire? You could get yourself into real trouble."

A strange idea came into my mind. "*You* didn't set the place on fire, did you, Neddy?"

He said, "Oh, use your brain. What would I do that for? I want to preserve things, not destroy them."

"But somebody must have started the fire," said Jake. "An empty building wouldn't catch light all by itself. Think of all the ways fires get started by accident – cigarette ends, chip pans, sparks from a fireplace…"

"Faulty wiring," said Neddy. "Leaking gas pipes."

"None of those could happen in an empty building," Jake said. "So the fire can't have started by accident. Someone did it on purpose."

"Not necessarily," said Neddy. "Cigarette ends – that could be accidental."

"In an empty building?"

Neddy said, "You've already proved that it's possible to get inside one of these places. If you can do it, so could other people. Perhaps they were simply careless."

"Yeah," said Jake. "They carelessly sloshed petrol around and carelessly dropped a match on it. Or else they decided to have a bonfire indoors, for a change."

I said, "I bet I know who it was – Greg and his gang. Don't you think it's strange that Greg isn't here? He seems to like watching fires. And half the town must have seen the smoke from this one."

People were still arriving, but they had missed the best of the action. The smoke was even thicker by now; the smell of it filled the air. But the flames had completely died down. An ambulance which had arrived, just in case, went away empty.

The brick walls of the warehouse were still standing. Through the gaps where the windows had been, you could see the sky. "Those walls will have to come down," said Jake. "They won't be able to leave the place in a state like that."

"Good. It will save the marina people some work," I said to annoy Neddy. But he didn't have a chance to reply. His grandmother had pushed her way through the crowd.

"Edward! It's time we were going. Remember, we've got work to do."

She handed him two of the bags she was carrying, and marched him off down Basin Street. He looked over his shoulder once or twice, as if to check we weren't following him.

"Interesting," I said. "Now where did she suddenly appear from? And where was Neddy when he spotted the fire?"

We began to head for home. Jake said, "They're quite mysterious, those two. I wonder what was in those bags she was carrying."

"I can tell you what *wasn't* in them," I said. "Shoes for Neddy. By the way, why can't a car play football?"

"I dunno."

"Because it's only got one boot."

"Oh, yeah. You've told me that one before."

"How come you didn't remember it, then?"

"I don't *want* to remember jokes like that. You know what Neddy says? The human brain is like a computer, and in your case the hard disk will soon be totally full. Not with useful information – with jokes. I'd rather fill my memory with useful stuff."

"Such as? What's the capital of Peru? What's the

French for 'donkey'? Who was king 500 years ago, and what did he die of? Jokes are far more useful, *I* think."

I found out years ago that jokes can be useful. When I was little, just starting school, I used to be quite shy – but I found that people would listen to me if I had a joke to tell. Even if they groaned instead of laughing, at least they noticed me.

A joke can fill a silence, or change an awkward conversation. A joke can turn people's anger away. (You have to time it right, though, or you make them even angrier.)

Most people can't remember more than half a dozen jokes. I am the only person I know who can remember hundreds. Maybe I'll be a comedian when I grow up, or write a joke book. That's another thing jokes can do – make you famous. And anyway, who needs to know the capital of Peru?

When I got home, Grace was in the kitchen. She was making sandwiches for Dad, who was still working hard on the garden. He had moved the rockery from the left-hand side to the right, and now he was re-laying a path.

Grace wrinkled her nose when I came in. "Yuk. You smell awful – all smoky. Even worse than Hannah."

I suddenly remembered that it was Hannah's day off from her shop. If Greg's gang had really set fire to the warehouse, Hannah could have been there too.

"Does Hannah smell smoky, then?" I said, trying to sound as if it wasn't important.

"She did when she came in. Then she had a bath and got changed. I bet her and Tanya have been smoking again," Grace said, and giggled.

But I didn't feel the least bit like laughing.

Chapter 12

What's the difference between a buffalo and a bison?

You can't wash your hands in a buffalo.

On Saturday the protest march went right through the town. It was much bigger than I'd expected. Jake and I watched as it made its way down Pump Street.

There were people from lots of different groups, each behind their own banner. Friends of the Planet, the Society for the Protection of Birds, England's Heritage, the Westhaven Society, the school Nature Club, Save the Whales…

"Save the Whales?" said Jake, surprised. "I've never heard of whales in the Basin."

"No. They'd need a bath-tub at least," I agreed.

Then came the Wetlands Protection Group, Historic Harbours, the Union of Licensed Victuallers…

"Pub-owners, that means," Jake explained. "They don't want another pub opening up in town. They think it will take away their customers."

The line seemed endless. At last we saw Neddy and his grandmother, marching behind a banner I'd never seen before. WAM! (*Westhaven Against Marina*, it said in smaller letters.)

I waved to Neddy. He waved back, looking faintly

embarrassed. His grandmother marched along, soldier-like, totally ignoring us.

Nobody cheered the marchers, but nobody booed them, either. There was something overpowering about the sight of so many people, all striding along with the same purpose in mind. Even though I didn't agree with them, I could not help feeling impressed.

I said so to Neddy the next day, as we sat in the minibus on the way to camp.

"Impressed, were you?" he said. "I only hope the Town Council felt the same. But somehow I don't think they did."

"Why not?"

"A march like that – it's not news. It doesn't get mentioned on TV or in the papers, except the *Westhaven Weekly*, and who takes any notice of that? We need to get more publicity. We need to take more drastic action! The time for marching is over!" He sounded as if he was repeating something he'd heard in a speech.

"What d'you mean by drastic action?" I asked.

"Never you mind. I keep forgetting you're the enemy. Stop asking questions, or else I'll have to shoot you for spying."

A noisy fight was breaking out in the seats behind us. Andy stopped the minibus with a screech of brakes, and the car behind almost ran into us. (Luckily we knew the people – they were going to the camp with us.)

"Stop it!" yelled Andy. "I can't drive with that row going on. If you can't be quiet, I'll have to separate you. You can travel in the cars instead of the minibus."

That shut them up. It was Darren and Macaulay who

had started the fight – no surprise there. They both live near us. Darren's not too bad if he's by himself, but he often hangs around with Macaulay's lot, who are just plain trouble.

Darren and Macaulay had been coming to the Friday Club now and then. They usually left before the talk at the end; if they did stay for it, they would mess around, distract other people and annoy Andy. I bet he wasn't too pleased when they put their names down for the camp.

I wasn't too pleased, either, to find they were sharing a tent with Neddy and me. Maybe Andy thought we would be a good influence on them. Some chance!

As soon as we arrived, they started causing trouble. They grumbled about the camp site – well, okay, it was a field rather than a camp site, with no buildings except the toilet and shower block. It was in a quiet valley, surrounded by woods. The nearest town was four miles away.

"I thought it would be a proper camp site," Darren muttered. "With a club-house and a swimming pool and a games arcade and that. This is boring."

"Why didn't you go to Butlins' instead?" said Neddy.

Macaulay said, "Four days in this dump! What are we going to do? We'll be bored stupid."

"Last year," I said, "we did things like canoeing and rock-climbing, and played football a lot. And there was this game we played in the woods - it was really good. Nobody got bored."

"How old are you, kid?" said Macaulay. "Ten? Eleven?"

"Eleven."

"Well, I'm thirteen. I don't find it exciting playing kids' games in the woods. What did you play at, the Teddy Bears' Picnic?"

Darren sniggered. The two of them went off among the trees, although we were all supposed to be helping to put the tents up. Just as we were finishing, it started to rain. Quickly we shoved our backpacks and sleeping bags into the tent.

"It would serve those two right if we left their things outside to get wet," said Neddy. "They might catch pneumonia and have to go to hospital, and then we'd get some peace." But he helped me move their bags under cover – not that we got any thanks for it.

"Who's moved my bag?" said Macaulay when he came back. His voice was angry.

"Us. We'll put it back where we found it, if you insist," said Neddy. "But most people prefer a dry sleeping bag to a soaking wet one."

"Just don't touch it again, all right?" Macaulay said menacingly. I wondered what he'd got in there that he didn't want us to see. Cigarettes? Rude photos? Cans of lager?

I thought of a joke. "What's round and bad-tempered?"

Nobody answered.

"A vicious circle," I said.

"Or Macaulay's face," suggested Neddy.

"Are you asking for a punch in the gob?" said Macaulay.

It could have got nasty, but just then the whistle blew for supper. We had to eat it in the marquee because it was still raining. Needless to say, Darren and Macaulay didn't think much of the food, and said so. But Neddy and I kept well out of their way.

After supper, Andy's wife Sue stood up to give a talk. I noticed the Terrible Two slide out of the marquee – they were probably going out in the woods for a quick smoke.

Later, when Neddy and I went back to our tent, we were surprised to find them already in their sleeping bags. Darren gave an enormous fake yawn. "We were *so* tired," he said. "Must be all this fresh air."

"Or it was fresh," said Macaulay, "until Darren took his boots off."

They sounded quite friendly. They must be up to something.

It was dark by now. We got ready for bed by torchlight. Neddy slid into his sleeping bag – then leapt out again with a startled yell.

"What's the matter?"

"There's something in my sleeping bag!"

He shook the bag, and something fell out. It was a small frog, quite dead, its legs spread out stiffly.

"I know you're keen on nature and that, Neddy," said Darren. "But why can't you leave your pets at home?"

"How very childish of someone," Neddy said calmly. "Mental age of about six, I'd say." He opened the tent flap and lobbed the frog out into the darkness. We heard a sudden piercing scream.

"Aaaaaargh! A bat! I felt a bat in my hair!"

One of the girls must have been passing at just the wrong moment. She sounded quite hysterical – and so were Darren and Macaulay. Hysterical with laughter.

Cautiously I shook my sleeping bag upside down. Nothing came out, but it seemed to feel rather odd…

cold and heavy. It was soaking wet.

"Oh, great," I said. "The tent must be leaking."

"Excuses, excuses," said Macaulay. "You're only a kid. I suppose it's not surprising if you wet the bed sometimes." And they went off into fits of laughter again.

"You did this! You idiots! What am I supposed to sleep in tonight?"

Darren said, "Calm down, Ben. Where's that famous sense of humour? Can't you take a joke?"

Neddy was angry now. He grabbed the bottom of Darren's sleeping bag and tried to shake Darren out of it. Darren yelled and held on. Macaulay, shouting his head off, grabbed Neddy's ankles; I whacked Macaulay round the head with the wet sleeping bag. Somehow one of the tent poles got knocked out of place, and the tent began to cave in.

"What on earth is going on?"

It was Andy, sounding tired and cross. He told us all off – which was quite unfair. (Neddy and I hadn't started it, after all.) Then he said that if we kept on fighting we would have to have an adult sleeping in our tent. Of course, none of us wanted that.

Andy fixed the tent and found me a spare sleeping bag to use. When he'd gone, I lay awake for a long time. In the other tents I could hear people talking quietly and sometimes laughing; but in our tent there was a stony silence. I never knew that silence could sound more angry than a shout.

Chapter 13

Why was Cinderella useless at tennis?

Because her coach was a pumpkin.

The next day, the Terrible Two began their little games all over again. My spare trainers mysteriously vanished; so did Neddy's knife, fork and spoon. Of course we knew who was responsible – but we didn't want to start another fight.

"Somehow we must divert their attention," said Neddy. "Give them something else to think about. They're only misbehaving because they're bored; that's what Grandmother always says."

"Oh? And what would your grandmother recommend?"

His face took on the blank kind of look which means he's had an idea. But he wouldn't tell me what it was – typical. "You'll know all right if it's success-ful," he said.

At least the rain had stopped. I spent the morning playing football and volleyball. Neddy, who excels at everything else, is hopeless at ball games (because of his asthma, he says – but I reckon that's just an excuse). Instead, he went bird-watching in the woods.

We didn't see much of Darren and Macaulay, but at lunchtime Neddy went to sit beside them. I saw him whisper something to them.

"What did you tell them?" I asked him later.

"You won't approve. I had to bend the truth a little… well, quite a lot actually."

"Oh, go on. Tell me."

"Only that I overheard Sophie and Charlotte talking about boys. I told Macaulay that Sophie likes him."

"He didn't *believe* you, did he?" Sophie and Charlotte are both quite good-looking – if you like the sort of girl who giggles a lot. But Macaulay's no oil painting, and neither is Darren.

Neddy said, "He swallowed every word of it. Just like Darren, when I told him that Charlotte fancies him."

"No! They're either big-headed or stupid. Or both."

Macaulay and Darren spent the entire day trying to chat up Sophie and Charlotte. Even more surprising – the girls seemed to like it.

"Neddy, you're a genius," I said.

"Yes, I know." He smiled modestly.

The next day, things were still quite calm. We went to visit the local town, Shilmouth, where we had fish and chips for lunch. In the afternoon we went canoeing.

"How many people have been in a canoe before?" asked Andy. All the people who had been to last year's camp put their hands up, including me. To my surprise, Neddy's hand went up too. "I learned in Norway," he told me, "on a bird-watching holiday."

"Don't worry if you've never tried it," said Andy. "The water's very shallow, and Mr Jones and I will teach you." (Mr Jones was the owner of the canoes we were hiring.) "The people who feel confident in a canoe can go off on their own, as long as they don't go too far away. Don't go up river beyond the bridge, and don't go down river beyond… where shall we say, Mr Jones?"

"No further than the Palace," said Mr Jones. "That's the white building, down river on the opposite side. Everybody see it? Don't go beyond it. This is a tidal river, and when the tide turns there's quite a flow of water going out beyond that point. If you're not careful you could get swept right out to sea."

Andy said, "Did everyone hear that?" and people nodded. "Okay. Be back here by three or we'll leave without you!"

I shared a canoe with Neddy. I got in carefully – that's the bit I don't like because it feels so wobbly. It's all right once you're in and sitting down. We made a quick getaway, just in case the Terrible Twins felt like following us. But they only had eyes for Sophie and Charlotte, who were with the beginners' group, giggling like mad as their canoe rocked about.

The tide was at its highest, which meant that the water had almost stopped flowing. The river looked more like a lake, broad and calm. We went down river, between low grassy banks where sheep were grazing. It was very peaceful; we had left the boathouse and the town behind us. We had also left most of the others behind, because Neddy was setting quite a fast pace.

Soon my arms began to ache. It was hard work keeping up with Neddy. (In a two-seater canoe, you have to work in time with the person in front, or else you keep hitting his paddle.) "Can we stop for a minute? My arms need a rest," I panted.

The canoe glided on slowly. We were about half-way to the white building which Mr Jones had called the Palace.

"I wonder what that place is?" said Neddy. "It looks like a hotel or something. Funny place to build one, though, all on its own like that."

We were still moving along, although no one was paddling. The tide must have turned. Slowly it carried us down river like a drifting leaf; the white building drew nearer and nearer.

"We're not allowed to go past there," I reminded Neddy.

"I know. But he never said we couldn't go up to it, did he?" Neddy began to paddle again. He brought us in towards the river bank beside the tall white building. We bumped gently against a wooden quay.

Now that we were close to it, we could see that the building was more like a ruin than a palace. Windows were broken, doors hung loose; all the white paint was flaking off. We could just about read the weather-beaten sign, PALACE YACHT CLUB.

"Strange," said Neddy. "It's not an old building. The architecture is quite modern. Why has it all gone to ruin like that?"

The canoe gave a little lurch, as if it had touched the river bottom. Of course, the tide was going out. "We'd better get moving," I said, "or we'll be left high and dry."

"And that's another odd thing," said Neddy, as we headed out across the river. "That quay looks as if it was designed for boats much bigger than a canoe. But they would never be able to reach it – the water's too shallow."

"Oh-oh," I said. "Look who's coming."

Another canoe was speeding towards us, powered along by Darren and Macaulay. (We found out later that Sophie and Charlotte had rocked the boat one time too often. They had capsized, soaked themselves and gone off to get dry.) With the outgoing tide to help them, the Terrible Two were racing along. We had to swerve out of their way.

"We're not supposed to go further than this," I called to them.

"Who says?"

"The owner."

"He was talking about kids like you. Not experts like us two," said Darren.

"See you later," Macaulay called over his shoulder. They went past the Palace and round a corner, where the river channel narrowed. The grassy bank hid them from our sight.

"Morons," said Neddy. "They'll find it much harder work coming back, with the tide and the river against them."

"Well, they can't say nobody warned them. Is it time we headed back now?"

Neddy looked at his watch. "Not yet. I want to have a closer look at that Palace. We could land over there, I think – where the banks are lower."

We slid the canoe onto a sort of muddy beach, which was getting wider as the tide went out. It was a messy landing. Our feet sank into the mud, and I nearly lost a trainer. But at last we were on solid ground.

"What if somebody steals the canoe?" I said anxiously.

"Hide the paddles under those bushes, if you're worried," said Neddy. "But there's no one about."

He was right. This side of the river, away from the

town, was an empty landscape of open fields, populated only by sheep. Farther down river, two women were walking their dogs; there was no one else in sight.

A rough road, full of pot-holes, led towards the Palace. When we got closer it was even more depressing than it had looked from the water. In the car park weeds were growing through the tarmac. Inside, there was broken glass and rubbish on the floor, and a smell like an old, filthy toilet. Disgusting as it was, we found signs that someone – a tramp, perhaps – had been living there.

"Yuk," I said. "But it must have looked pretty smart when it was new. I wonder what happened?"

We came out, glad to breathe fresh air again.

"Hey, you boys!" a voice called. It was a woman with a dog. "You shouldn't go in there – it's dangerous. The whole place might fall down on you."

"Don't worry," I said, "we're not going back in. It smells."

"Thank you for the warning," said Neddy in his most polite voice, the one he uses at home. "I wonder if you could satisfy our curiosity. What happened to the place? Why has it gone to ruin like this?"

"Oh, it's a long story," the woman said. "Big ideas, they had, but it all came to nothing, and it cost the town a fortune."

"Am I right in thinking that it was built as a yacht club?" said Neddy.

"That's right. They had to dredge the river bed to make it deep enough for yachts to come in. Ten or twelve years ago, this was, and at first things went well. The place was popular, it brought people into the town. But all the time the river was doing what rivers always do... washing down silt and mud."

"Couldn't they dredge it out again?" I said.

"Of course they could, but it all cost money. The club wasn't making enough to pay for it. About five years ago they went bankrupt, and that was the end of it all. Nothing left except that building, which is neither use nor ornament, and a lot of money owing to people in the town."

Neddy said to me, "That's exactly what could happen with the marina. Why didn't I bring my camera? The whole of Westhaven ought to see this place."

"Don't talk rubbish," I said. "This has got nothing to do with the marina."

"It's got everything to do with it. Have Grandfield done their sums properly? Do they know that dredging the Basin once may not be enough? They might have to do it every year, every six months…"

I said to the woman, "Who were the people who built this place? They weren't called Grandfield Enterprises, were they?"

She shook her head. "Greeves and Cotrill was the company name. And if Mr Greeves or Mr Cotrill ever show their faces in Shilmouth again, they'll wish they hadn't."

But Neddy wasn't listening. "Something's wrong," he said, pointing down river.

The other lady, with her dog, was hurrying towards us. She was quite stout. She could only run a few paces at a time, then she had to walk, but clearly she was going as fast as she could. She looked frightened.

"Marjorie! Whatever's the matter?"

"Two boys," she panted. "In a canoe. They've been washed out to sea."

Chapter 14

How does a boat cut through the waves?

With a sea-saw.

"It must be Darren and Macaulay," I said. "I can't believe they would be so stupid."

"Can't you? I can," said Neddy. "What do we do now?"

"Dial 999 for the coastguard and they'll call the lifeboat," said the first lady. "But it's a mile to the nearest phone. Are you boys good runners? You need to go up river as far as the bridge, cross over, take the first left –"

"The boathouse is nearer," said Neddy.

"But that's on the opposite side of the river," panted the stout lady.

"It's okay. We've got a canoe. Come on, Ben!"

We raced back to where we'd left the canoe, slid it down the muddy beach and squelched after it.

"The paddles! Don't forget the paddles!"

For one horrible moment I thought I'd hidden them too well, but then I found them. I climbed into the canoe, not caring how wet or muddy I got. We began to paddle upstream as fast as we could.

It was hard work with the tide against us. "Keep in to the side," said Neddy. "The current won't be so strong."

My arms began to ache again. I gritted my teeth and kept on paddling in time with Neddy. Hurry, hurry. Mustn't stop. Mustn't stop.

Oh God, please help us to get there quickly. Please help the lifeboat to find them. Let the sea be calm, don't let the canoe capsize. And help Darren and Macaulay not to panic. Even though they've been really stupid, they don't deserve to drown…

We could see the boathouse now, and we steered towards it. Crossing the river, we could feel the current trying to pull us off course. I dug in harder with my left-hand paddle, fighting the strength of the tide. My arms felt ready to drop off.

At last we were there. We gabbled out the story to Andy; his face turned white.

"Ring the coastguard," said Mr Jones. "The phone's in my office. I'll take a boat out and look for them – might save a bit of time."

He ran along the quayside to where a motor-boat was moored. Soon it was roaring down the river and out of sight. Several minutes later the Shilmouth lifeboat shot past us. It was a small inflatable, going so fast that it seemed to bounce over the water.

By now all the other canoes had come back. People stood around in little groups, not saying much, just waiting… waiting…

At last Andy and Sue decided that most of us should go back to the camp site. Andy would wait at the boathouse. As we climbed silently into the minibus, we heard a helicopter fly low overhead.

"Air-sea rescue," said Neddy.

"Does that mean they've been found?" I asked.

"Maybe. Or maybe it means the lifeboat can't find them."

I said, because the thought had been bothering me, "Do you think we should have reported them as soon as they went down river?"

"Told on them, you mean? They would have killed us."

Yes. And we had tried to warn them. But they hadn't believed us – until it was too late.

Supper was being dished up, although no one felt very hungry, when Andy came back. He was alone. But as he leapt out of the car, we could see that he was smiling.

"They're safe! They've been found!" he cried.

There was a babble of excited voices. What happened? Where are they? Did the helicopter have to winch them up, like on TV?

Andy explained, "The helicopter found them two miles out to sea, and the lifeboat picked them up. The canoe had capsized – luckily they managed to cling onto it. They were in the water for over an hour. They're in hospital because they're both suffering from shock. But the doctor says they'll be okay."

"Will they be coming back to camp?" asked Sophie.

"I don't think so. Their parents are coming to the hospital – they'll probably take them home tomorrow." Was that relief on Andy's face?

Sophie and Charlotte looked quite upset. Their holiday romance had come to a sudden end. (But why on earth did they like Macaulay and Darren? I will never understand girls.)

With a much better appetite – even though the food

had gone cold – we finished our supper.

I said to Neddy, "There's this little kid, and he says to his teacher, 'Miss, I eated six fish fingers today.' She says, 'Ate, Jack. Ate.' And he goes, 'Well, it might have been eight, miss. All I know is, I eated a lot.'"

Neddy sighed. "I wondered how long it would be before you started up again. Ben, I know you like collecting jokes, but do you have to tell them all the time? Can't you just enjoy them in private? Laugh at them secretly, inside your head?"

I felt hurt. "Don't you like hearing new jokes?"

"Yes – if they're funny. And if you haven't told them to me three times already."

"That is a problem," I admitted. "I can remember the jokes all right, I just can't remember who's already heard them."

Neddy said, "Look, I enjoy birdwatching, but I don't bring birds into the conversation all the time. If I did, people would soon get bored, wouldn't they?"

"Are you saying I ought to stop telling jokes?"

"Not stop altogether. Just cut down a bit. Otherwise you'll end up like my great-uncle Reggie."

"Who?"

"Grandmother's little brother. He's 62 and he behaves like a ten-year-old. Playing silly tricks on people – whoopee cushions and fake spiders and things. Telling jokes all the time, especially when people are trying to hold a serious conversation. Grandmother says it's attention-seeking behaviour."

I thought about this. It was true, I had started telling jokes as a way of getting attention, when I was new at school and felt shy. But now, my jokes were a part of me. Ben the joker – that was how people saw me. I had a reputation to live up to.

I wasn't clever like Neddy or adventurous like Jake. If I stopped telling jokes, would anyone ever notice me at all? Would they think I was totally boring and ordinary? Would I ever find anything interesting to say?

Neddy said, "You could try being a bit more choosy. Don't tell every joke that pops into your head – just the really good ones."

Suddenly I felt angry. "And *you* could try minding your own business," I said. "I like telling jokes. If you don't want to hear them, cover your ears."

He laughed. It didn't even cross his mind that he might have hurt me by what he'd said. That's Neddy – clever most of the time, but sometimes really dense.

Later, as Andy gave the usual evening talk in the marquee, I found it hard to concentrate. Did other people feel the same way as Neddy? Were they annoyed, not amused, by my jokes? Perhaps I should try to cut down a bit... only tell the best ones. (But often, you don't know if people will like a joke until you try it out on them. Different people laugh at different things.)

The words "Darren and Macaulay" caught my attention. I realised that Andy was talking about what had happened earlier.

"They broke the rules," he said. "They thought it wouldn't matter. They thought they were so good at canoeing, they wouldn't come to any harm. I wonder what they felt like as the current swept them out to sea?

"At first they probably thought they could fight it. They paddled harder and harder, but still the tide was pulling them away from the land. Their arms got tired. They were exhausted. And by now they were in the open sea. Waves were rocking the boat, and each wave was bigger than the last one. Then an extra-big wave tipped them over.

"They couldn't manage to get back in the canoe. All they could do was to cling onto it. They couldn't save themselves – their only hope was to wait for someone who would rescue them.

"But don't be too hard on Macaulay and Darren. Okay, so they broke the rules – but we've all done that. We've all broken some very important rules, the rules God gave us. Is there anyone here who can say you've never told a lie? Never hurt anyone? Never hated someone? Never disobeyed your parents?

"We've all done it. We've all broken God's rules, and every time we do that, we get further away from God, like a boat drifting further away from the land. And we can't get back – not on our own. I don't know if you've ever told yourself that you're going to be really good from now on. You're going to stop telling lies, stop losing your temper, stop trying to kill your kid brother... But it doesn't work, does it? You can be good for a short while, but then the old habits come back, too strong for you to fight. Like the tide carrying you back out to sea.

"But God loves us, even though we've broken the rules. He hates to see us drifting further and further away from him. He knows we can't save ourselves, and so he sent out a lifeboat to rescue us.

"I'm talking about Jesus. God sent Jesus into the world so that we can be saved. We can be rescued and brought back to the safety of the shore – back to God."

I glanced at Neddy, wondering what he was thinking. But his face gave nothing away. His eyes were fixed on Andy.

"There are some people," Andy went on, "who don't want to be rescued. They feel quite happy paddling their own canoe… running their own lives, making their own decisions. They don't feel any need to believe in God, and sometimes it takes a major problem – like a wave overturning a boat – to make them realise they need to be rescued.

"But you don't have to wait until that happens. If you want to be saved, if you want to come back to God, then the lifeboat is just waiting to pick you up. All you have to do is get on board. How? Well, you could pray this prayer with me. You don't have to say it aloud, because God knows the thoughts of your heart.

"Dear God, I know I've broken your rules, and I'm sorry. I want to come back to you. Please save me, through Jesus, your Son. Amen."

There was a moment of silence, apart from the patter of rain on the roof.

"If anyone prayed that prayer tonight," said Andy, "then please come and tell me. It always helps to tell someone. Everyone else – it's time for bed."

I got up, but Neddy stayed put.

"You go on," he said. "I want to talk to Andy."

"Oh. Do you mean… did you…?"

He nodded. "I suppose that means I'm a Christian now." Suddenly a huge smile lit up his face. "Be honest. You never thought it would happen to me, did you?"

Chapter 15

*Which game is played using eighteen
people and one phone box?*

Squash.

Neddy was right – I never really thought it would
happen to him. After all, Neddy was the one who used
to laugh at me for believing in God. He was always
asking smart questions that I couldn't answer. He used
to say he believed in some kind of Life Force which
created the universe – but he couldn't believe in the
Christian God.

So what had changed his mind?

"Lots of things," he said.

We were lying in our tent. It was nice and peaceful
– no Darren and Macaulay to disturb us, just Neddy
and me talking quietly in the dark.

"Like what?" I asked.

"Like when I prayed about something, and it happened. Like seeing how people change when they start
believing in God. And then tonight – I can't explain it
really… something happened to me tonight."

He paused, trying to think of the right words. Neddy
at a loss for words! This was something new, all right.

"When Andy was talking," he said, "I suddenly…
well, I felt that… I sort of knew that God wanted to tell

me something. It was that bit about people who don't want to be rescued, who think they're managing okay on their own. Well, that was me. I didn't want to believe in God because I wanted to be in charge of my own life. I didn't want anyone else telling *me* what to do…

"But then I thought, what if God actually does exist? What if I really am drifting away from him?

"So I decided the scientific thing would be to give God a try. I prayed that prayer along with Andy, and then… this is the bit I can't describe…"

He paused again. I heard him take a deep breath.

"All at once I just knew it was true. Everything. God does exist, and he knows me, and cares about me. It's amazing! And I feel so happy! I've never felt like this in my entire life." Even in the darkness I could tell that he was smiling.

I said nothing. I was feeling rather envious. After all, I had prayed that prayer, or one very like it, years ago in Sunday School. But I hadn't felt the kind of happiness Neddy was talking about.

Perhaps I wasn't really a Christian, then? Perhaps that was why I never seemed to hear God's voice speaking to me, the way Grace and Neddy had. Maybe Hannah was right – I only called myself a Christian because Mum and Dad had brought me up that way.

Instead of being pleased about Neddy, I felt confused. If only I could talk to someone like Andy…

But the next day was a busy one, with a swimming trip in the morning and abseiling in the afternoon. And the day after that was the last day of camp. We packed up the tents, loaded the minibus and got ready to leave.

"Well, Ben? Have you enjoyed yourself?" said Andy.

"Most of the time. But I wanted to ask you something –"

"Andy!" called Sue. "Where shall I put the saucepans?"

It wasn't the moment for a serious talk. I sat down beside Neddy, who was still far too happy himself to notice that I was rather quiet.

"What have I missed, then?" I said to Dad. He was reading the jobs section of the *Westhaven Weekly* and looking depressed. "Anything startling happen while I was away?"

"Not much," he said gloomily.

"What's that about? Fire in a school?"

Dad snatched the paper away. "Wait till I've finished, can't you?" he muttered.

"It was nothing serious," said Grace. "Some kids – at least they think it was kids – set fire to a shed at Lime Street School. Nobody got hurt, and they didn't manage to burn down the school."

"There seem to have been a lot of fires in Westhaven recently." I said it loudly because Hannah was standing in the doorway. But she didn't react at all.

"Dad, I'm going round Tanya's," she said. "See you later."

"Not too much later. I want you back here by ten at the very latest," Dad said. "Did you hear me?"

"Aw but Dad, Tanya's got this video – "

"I said, did you hear me?" Dad roared. He was very irritable these days.

"I heard," said Hannah sulkily.

Mum came in, looking weary because she'd done the shopping on her way back from work. I went to help her unload it.

"Did you get some fruit juice, Mum?" I asked. "We're right out of it."

"No, love. Sorry. I've decided that we'll have orange squash instead. It's cheaper and it lasts a lot longer."

I hate orange squash. But I knew it was no use complaining.

While we were at camp, I had almost stopped worrying about things at home – there was too much else to think about. But now I was starting to feel anxious again.

"Mum," I said, "we are all right for money, aren't we? I mean, with your job, and the rent from the flat?"

She pushed the hair back from her face. (She hadn't had a haircut in months, I realised. Her hair was getting long and untidy and it didn't suit her.)

"Well, we're managing, just about," she said. "We're keeping our heads above water. But it will be nice when your dad finds work again – and he will, don't you worry. We just have to wait and be patient."

"Do *you* never get worried, Mum?"

"Of course I get worried. I have to keep reminding myself that God is looking after us…"

"That's what Grandad says. *Leave all your worries with him, because he cares for you.*" I had learnt it by heart.

Mum smiled. "If Grandad can manage to do that, then surely we can too." I knew what she meant. At least, unlike Granny, we were all fit and healthy and in our right minds.

"How does Grandad manage it?" I said. "How does he go on trusting in God, and staying so calm, and not worrying?"

Mum said, "I suppose it's because he's had a lifetime of practice. He's seen bad times and good times. He knows the bad times won't last for ever. He knows that everything changes... except God himself. God is the same yesterday, and today, and for ever."

Like a rock, I thought. And a kind of picture came into my mind – a great rock, with waves washing around it and storms beating it. But the rock was far stronger than waves or wind.

There were people standing on the rock. *They* could feel the power of the storm, and sometimes they were frightened. But the ground was firm beneath them. As long as they stayed on the rock, they were safe.

But how could I know – really know for certain – that my own feet were on the rock?

Chapter 16

How do cows talk to each other?

On moobile phones.

Next day, when I went to call on Neddy, there was no one at home. Late in the afternoon I saw a battered old Land Rover pull up outside his house. Neddy got out of the back, and his grandmother climbed stiffly out of the passenger seat. She was carrying a camera.

"Thank you, Roy," she said to the driver, a youngish man with a thin beard and a camouflage jacket. I vaguely recognised him, perhaps from the protest march.

"See you tonight, then," said Roy. "Let's hope we get a result."

"Hi, Neddy," I said. "Where have you been all day?"

"Shilmouth."

"But we only got back from there yesterday!"

"True." He was being all mysterious again.

"Edward!" said Mrs Fortescue. "We don't have much time. Could you take this film to be developed? Ask for the fast service, and wait until it's ready. Hurry, now. We shall need the pictures tonight."

What was happening that night? I found out from Dad. There was to be a public meeting at the Town

Hall, to discuss the marina project and answer people's questions.

"Can I go?"

"No. The place will be full of fanatics and weirdos – I wouldn't be surprised if there's trouble."

I wondered how Neddy's grandmother would react to that. Fanatic? Weirdo? How dare you! Write out 1000 times, *I must respect my elders and betters.*

"Are you going to go, Dad?" I asked.

"I might."

But in the end he couldn't be bothered. He seemed to have lost all his energy. He'd finished reorganising the garden, and now, with nothing else to do, he spent most of his time slumped in front of the TV. (This was driving Mum crazy. She thought he should be helping with the housework, instead of leaving it all to her when she got in from work.)

The morning after, I heard from Neddy how the meeting had gone. "The hall was packed," he said. "At least half were on our side – I mean against the marina."

"And the other half?" I said.

"The other half consisted of idiots like you, who think the marina will improve the town, or help them find work, or reduce their Council Tax. Crazy! Increase their Council Tax, more likely. The Council are planning to give Grandfield a huge loan towards the cost of the work. Just like at Shilmouth. And it could all be money down the drain... or down the river."

"Those photos you brought back from Shilmouth – I suppose they were of the Palace?"

"Right. We got some good ones at low tide,

showing the Sailing Club surrounded by acres of mud. But we never got the chance to use them. Grandmother managed to ask a question… 'Are the Council aware of a similar scheme at Shilmouth, which went bankrupt when the moorings silted up?' The Mayor and the Councillors all looked blank. Obviously they'd never heard of it. But then your Ferrari man stepped in."

"Mr Lewis?"

"Yes. He was there, with several others from Grandfield, all as smooth and smart as he is. He said Grandfield had studied lots of schemes around the country, successes *and* failures, and had learned from other people's mistakes. The Basin was not the same as the River Shil. The Basin would not need to be dredged more than once every ten years at the most.

"Somebody shouted out, 'Who says so?' and he said that Grandfield had done a survey in detail. It was all in their report, which anyone was welcome to read. Then they moved on to talk about public footpaths or something."

"So it's all right," I said. "It couldn't happen here like at Shilmouth."

"No!" cried Neddy. "It's not all right! The survey was done by Grandfield. Surprise, surprise – it said what Grandfield want it to say. We're going to get another survey done by a different company, just to see if they're right. The trouble is, that will take time. And we don't have much time. Grandfield are only waiting for the Council to say yes; they want to start work right away."

"Good," I said. "I hope the Council does say yes."

"Then you're a moron. Haven't you heard a word I've been saying?"

"Listen, Neddy. I would be on your side if it wasn't for Dad. Look at him." I opened the sitting room door slightly. Dad was sprawled in front of the TV, still in his dressing gown although it was nearly lunch time. He hadn't shaved for two or three days. He looked terrible.

"See?" I said as I closed the door. "He's changed. He never used to be like this. What he needs is to be back at work."

"Yes, well…" said Neddy. He looked uncomfortable. "Okay. I'm sorry I called you a moron."

What? Neddy saying sorry? I nearly fell over.

He said quickly, "But that doesn't mean the marina should go ahead, just so that your dad can find work."

"I don't see how you're going to stop it," I said.

"Don't you?" He smiled. "You wait. You haven't heard the last of WAM."

I was taking Jerry for a walk after tea. As I left the house, the red Ferrari came smoothly to a stop by the kerb. It was a warm evening; the driver's window was open. Mr Lewis was talking on his mobile phone.

I don't think I would have paid any attention, except that one word caught my ear. It was "Shilmouth". And so, while Jerry sniffed around his favourite lamp-post, I found myself listening in.

"… and then someone mentioned Shilmouth. The Palace Sailing Club. You don't remember it? No, that would be before your time, I expect. A bit of a disaster… we left it to sink in its own mud.

"What? Oh no, no one made the connection. Don't worry, old chap, there's absolutely nothing to link us with Shilmouth. The holding company went bankrupt.

A year later, we quietly started up again with a new name, new board of directors, new everything..."

Jerry tugged at the lead. I let him pull me along the street, out of earshot. I had heard quite enough.

Grandfield Enterprises had a secret history. They were not as successful as they seemed to be. Under a different name, they had built the Palace Sailing Club – "a bit of a disaster" – and then abandoned it, owing money which they never repaid.

Would the same thing happen in Westhaven? Would they make a quick profit, and then, if things went wrong, simply disappear? Declare themselves bankrupt, leaving huge debts behind them?

Surely not. After all, the marina scheme was much bigger and more expensive than the Palace. Surely Grandfield would get things right this time. They wouldn't repeat the mistakes of the past.

I wondered if I should tell anyone what I had heard. But who? The Town Council? They wouldn't believe me. Neddy and his friends? *They* would believe me all right. They would try to find out more – dig out the dirt on Grandfield. And if they found any proof of shady dealings, what would happen?

No marina project – that's what would happen. No chance of work for Dad. And no more rent money from Mr Lewis.

It was too risky. I'd better keep quiet. I'd better forget I'd ever heard mention of the Palace. Palace – what Palace? Buckingham Palace? Crystal Palace?

The Palace Sailing Club, Shilmouth? No... never heard of it.

Chapter 17

What is green, has six legs, and would kill you if it fell on you out of a tree?

A snooker table.

Coming back from the walk with Jerry, I saw the Land Rover outside Neddy's house again. Roy, the owner, was helping Neddy to load things into the back of it. Sleeping bags, saucepans, boxes of food, a camping stove…

"Are you off on another trip, Neddy?" I asked.

"You might say that."

"Back to Shilmouth?"

"Oh no. Somewhere much closer to home."

Roy laid a warning hand on Neddy's arm. At once he was silent.

It wasn't until the following day that I found out exactly where they had gone. Jake came hurrying across the square.

"You'll never guess what Neddy and his friends have done."

"Kidnapped the Mayor?" I suggested. "Attacked the Marina Exhibition with an army of highly-trained seagulls?"

"Nearly as good. They've taken over a warehouse in Basin Street!"

"What do you mean, taken over?"

"They've moved in. They're living there. I heard it on the radio – they say they won't come out until there's been a proper survey of the Basin."

"But why? I mean, why move into the warehouse?"

"Think about it. Grandfield can't demolish it while they're in there... so they can't start building on the land."

"Let's go round and have a look," I said.

It was easy to see which warehouse was occupied – not the one Jake and I had explored, but another one, opposite. A huge banner hung between the upstairs windows. The big gateway leading into the yard had been bricked up with blocks of concrete.

"They must have done that in the night," I said, impressed.

"The place is almost like a castle," said Jake. "Hard to get into. Easy to defend."

I saw what he meant. The wall that ran all round the outside was three metres high and topped with barbed wire. There was only one small doorway into the yard, and that could easily be blocked from the inside. And the warehouse itself rose up like the keep of a castle, tall and grim. A sentry was looking out from the roof; the sun flashed on his binoculars.

A small crowd of people stood in the street. Was that a TV camera? Then I noticed a head looking over the wall. It was a woman I had never seen before. Unless she was ten feet tall, she must be standing on a ladder, or something.

She was talking about the marina project; her voice was angry. "Nobody knows what effects there will be in five or ten or twenty years' time. The Council can't see beyond the end of their noses. All they care about is the money the town will make. They've been bribed by Grandfield Enterprises! They've been blinded by money!"

"Can I ask how many people you have with you?" said a man.

He was only a reporter from the local paper, but she glared at him as if he was spying for the enemy.

"Enough," she said. "And we have supplies to last us for months, if necessary."

"Wow!" I said to Jake. "Does Neddy plan on staying there for months? What about school? It's the start of term in a couple of weeks."

"That's a thought. Is it too late to join him?"

Neddy had said that WAM needed more publicity – more attention from newspapers and TV. In that case they had done the right thing. The warehouse featured on local TV news and on the radio; it was even in the national papers.

Jake and I watched a TV interview with the Mayor, who said, "Why should a few fanatics be allowed to stand in the way of progress?" When the interviewer put the same question to the woman from WAM, she said, "We are not fanatics. We're just ordinary people from all walks of life. All different ages, too. Our youngest member is 12, our oldest is 68."

"That must be Neddy and his grandmother," I said. "I wonder if they're watching this?"

"They can't be," said Jake. "No electricity, remember?"

I tried to imagine what it would be like living in the old warehouse. "It must be kind of creepy at night," I said, "if they've only got torches and lamps."

"Smelly, too," said Jake. "Unless they managed to turn the water on."

"Perhaps they collect water from the Basin at high tide. They wouldn't be able to drink that, though. Did they take in hundreds of bottles of mineral water?"

"Oh look," said Jake. "It's Ferrari man."

Mr Lewis was being interviewed. He was standing in Basin Street with the warehouses behind him. "I can't imagine why anyone should object to our scheme," he said. "Look at these buildings. They're old, they're decrepit, they're positively dangerous. And we could replace them with a brand new, state-of-the-art Leisure Centre which would be the jewel in Westhaven's crown! I ask you, which would most people prefer?"

"I don't like that guy much," said Jake. "He's sort of… slimy. I don't trust him."

"What makes you say that?"

"Oh, sorry. I forgot he was living in your house. Do *you* like him?"

"I hardly know the man," I said.

I still hadn't told anyone about that phone conversation. It was on my mind a lot; I'd tried to forget it but I couldn't.

"I must go," said Jake. "It's Henry's night off. I'm supposed to be helping Dad in the kitchen."

"What fun. That reminds me – what's white, makes a humming noise and swims underwater?"

"I'm going. Bye."

"A fridge," I called after him. "I lied about it swimming underwater."

Grandad came in. It was the night when he slept at our house, to give him the chance of a good night's rest. Mum had already gone round to his place to look after Granny.

"Quiet here tonight," he said. "Where is everyone?"

"Grace is sleeping over at a friend's house, Hannah's out, and Dad's gone to Southampton."

"*Southampton*?" Grandad's voice made it sound like the South Pole.

"Yes. Some guy he used to work with has moved there, and he says there are jobs going. Dad's just gone to have a look around. He'll be back sometime tonight."

"That's a long way to travel to work," said Grandad. "Or is he thinking of moving house?"

"We don't want to move. But maybe we'll have to. Or else Dad could live in Southampton part of the time, and come home at weekends. Or maybe... oh, I don't know!"

"One more thing to worry about, eh, Ben?"

I nodded. "I have been trying not to worry – like you said. But it's not easy."

"I know, son. I know."

"Grandad," I said, "when you have to choose what to do, how do you know what's right? Sometimes at church, people say 'The Lord told me to do...' something or other. But I don't seem to hear God's voice like that. So how can I know what God wants me to do?"

Grandad said, "There are lots of ways God speaks to people. One is through the Bible. I can't count the number of times I've read something in the Bible that was exactly what I needed to know. Or else God can use other people to tell us things. Or sometimes he wants us to use our own common sense. But there *are* times when he speaks to people quite clearly – like a voice inside their mind."

"Has that ever happened to you?"

"Yes. A few times."

I said, "It's never happened to me."

"And that bothers you, does it?"

"Well… it's not only that…" I explained about Neddy at camp – how happy he had been when he became a Christian. I didn't remember ever feeling like that. Perhaps I wasn't really a Christian at all?

Grandad thought for a minute. "Feelings don't prove anything," he said. "We're all different. Some people are happy by nature; some aren't. Some feel really joyful when they come to know God, and some don't feel any different from usual. It's not happiness that proves you're a Christian."

"What does prove it, then?"

"The promise of Jesus. It's in the Bible. He said, *I will never turn away anyone who comes to me*. And I know you did come to him, because you told me about it. I think you were six years old – but that's old enough to understand. And ever since, I've watched you growing up as a Christian. Finding out more about God... getting to know him... obeying him..."

"Oh! So it doesn't depend on… on saying the right prayer, or having the right feelings, or whatever."

"No. It only depends on Jesus. If we want to belong to him, he'll never turn us away. We're only human; our feelings change from day to day. Sometimes I feel close to God and sometimes I don't. But he doesn't change. We can always rely on him."

"I understand… I think."

"Good." Grandad yawned; it was only nine o'clock, but he looked terribly tired. "And now, if you'll excuse me, I think I'll have an early night."

Chapter 18

Why did Einstein have his phone cut off?

Because he wanted to win the Nobel Prize.

I sat by myself in the quiet kitchen. Grandad was in bed; Hannah and Dad were still out. There wasn't a sound except for the tick of the clock and the soft purr of Tubs, the cat.

I felt happier after my talk with Grandad. But I still didn't know what to do about Mr Lewis. Should I tell anyone, or not? Would it make any difference if I did? After all, I had no proof of what I had heard him say.

Glancing across the kitchen, I noticed the door in the corner. It was bolted shut, and had been ever since Mr Lewis moved in. Behind it was a flight of stairs leading down to the flat. It would be so easy to slip down there and look around. I might find something that would help me decide what to do – papers, letters, anything at all about Grandfield or about Mr Lewis himself.

But what if he was at home? I ran to the front window. The red Ferrari was nowhere in sight, although there was plenty of parking space. He must be out.

Cautiously I slid back the bolt on the door. I went downstairs very slowly – because the stairs were old and creaky, but also because I had the uneasy feeling that perhaps I shouldn't be doing this.

That's stupid, I told myself. You're not a burglar – this is your own home.

But it's still wrong to mess about with somebody else's things. After all, you would be angry if Mr Lewis crept into *your* room. Wouldn't you?

Oh, shut up.

There was another door at the bottom of the stairs. Then I remembered that Dad had put a lock on that, too – on the other side. But perhaps Mr Lewis hadn't bothered to lock it.

I tried the door; it wouldn't move. All of a sudden I heard a sound that made my heart stand still: the sound of a key in a lock.

I froze, waiting for the door to swing open. But it didn't. The key must have opened the front door of the flat. Now I could hear footsteps and voices in the room beyond.

One was a voice I didn't know – a man's voice. "So this is your little hideaway? Slumming it a bit, aren't you? I thought you would have been at the Royal Hotel or the Grand."

Mr Lewis laughed. "How much do you think they pay me? Anyway, this place has its advantages. It's quite anonymous; no one notices my comings and goings. For that, I can put up with the Oxfam Shop furniture and the kids thumping about overhead."

I didn't dare to move – the creaking stairs would give me away. I almost didn't dare to breathe.

There were other noises: glasses clinking, drinks being poured. Then the stranger said, "So you talked to the boss? What did he say?"

"He agrees with me. We *must* get those protestors out of Basin Street. We can't afford any delay if we're to be up and running on time."

"Not to mention the bad publicity," said the other man.

Mr Lewis said, "Of course, it should be possible to get them evicted. But that will take time. It crossed my mind that there's a quicker way to get them out." He lowered his voice; I couldn't make out what he was saying.

"What?" The stranger sounded shocked. "Isn't that a bit extreme?"

"I don't think so. It may not work, of course. But if it doesn't, we haven't lost anything. We can still go through the legal process and evict them."

"I suppose so. But I don't like the sound of it. What if someone gets hurt?"

"Then they'll only have themselves to blame. Don't forget, they're breaking the law. They're occupying a derelict building. They're probably using paraffin lamps and camping stoves and all kinds of dangerous things. It's an accident waiting to happen – anyone can see that."

The other man did not answer.

"Well? Are you game for it, or not? Because if not, I shall be forced to tell the boss that you wouldn't cooperate."

"I'm game," the stranger said hastily. "When were you thinking of doing it?"

"Tonight, of course. I've got everything we need."

"Ben! What on earth do you think you're doing?"

The voice came from behind me. Hannah was looking through the open door at the top of the stairs.

I put my finger to my lips. She must have seen by my face how scared I was, for she kept quiet. She watched me as I climbed the stairs, treading as lightly as I could. At last I was at the top; I closed the door and bolted it.

"Wait till Dad hears about this," she said. "Spying on Mr Lewis! He'll go mad."

"Shut up," I said. "Is Dad home yet?"

"No."

I wished he would come back. He might know what to do – I certainly didn't.

"What's the matter?" said Hannah.

"There's something very weird going on." I told her what I had heard. "I don't know exactly what he's planning, but I don't like the sound of it. Even his friend thought it was risky."

"You ought to warn Neddy and his friends. Tell them to be extra watchful."

"Yes, but how? I can't exactly ring them up, can I? Or e-mail them?"

"No. You'd have to go there yourself."

I looked at the clock. It was nearly ten – I should have been in bed ages ago – and pitch dark outside. I really didn't want to go out there on my own, quite apart from what Dad would say when he knew about it.

I said, "I don't suppose you'd come with me, would you?"

"Okay," she said, to my surprise. "You know, I never have liked that man Lewis. He saw us once, down Basin Street. We weren't doing anything – well, only messing about – but he started shouting at us to get out. Greg said something cheeky – I thought the man was going to hit him. I wish he had! Greg would have taught him a lesson!"

"Come on," I said. "Let's go. Hey, do you think we should tell Grandad what's happening?"

"Are you crazy? Like Grandad's going to let us go down Basin Street at this time of night – sure. Anyway, he's asleep. We'll be back in half an hour, he won't miss us."

It was a warm night. In the town centre, people were sitting outside cafes or eating chips as they strolled along. Laughter and music spilled out from brightly-lit pubs.

Further on it was quieter; shops were closed, few people were about. Then we turned the corner into Basin Street, which was as dark and cold as outer space. Most of the street lights were unlit. A chill wind blew across the Basin, out of the vast emptiness of the night.

We passed the burned-out warehouse. Its outer walls were still standing; through gaps where the windows had been, the stars shone pale.

"I bet your friend Greg enjoyed doing that," I said.

"Doing what?"

"Setting light to that place."

"What *are* you on about?" she said.

"Didn't he start that fire? They say it was started on purpose."

"Maybe it was. But not by Greg."

I said, "How do you know?"

"Because I was with him that afternoon. We were up on the cliffs at Sheepstone – we saw the smoke in the distance. He was mad about missing it. He likes fires."

"I suppose he didn't start the fire at Lime Street School, either?"

"Ah, now that one he might have had something to do with. But he's not greedy. A shed, a bonfire – yes. But not a whole building."

I didn't argue, because by now we had reached the occupied warehouse. I could see the banner, a pale shape against the dark wall. But there were no other signs of life – no lights, no sounds. Were they all asleep?

We came to the small door that led into the yard. I tried it. It was firmly shut, probably barred on the inside.

"Hallo? Anyone there?"

No answer. I banged on the door; the sound made a hollow echo in the quiet street.

"Neddy? Are you there? Let us in! It's important!"

Only silence, and the wind moaning.

I put my shoulder hard against the door. It wouldn't budge. I knew we couldn't possibly climb the wall; it was too high, even without the vicious rows of barbed wire that leaned outward from the top of it.

"Neddy! Is anyone there?" I shouted.

"Maybe they've given up and gone home," said Hannah.

"Not Neddy. This is too important to him... No, they must all be in bed." I thought they were stupid not to have left someone on lookout through the night. But then, they didn't know about Mr Lewis. And they never would at this rate – until too late.

"There is another way in, you know," Hannah said. "At least I think there is."

"Where?"

"From over there." She pointed across the road to another warehouse – the one Jake and I had visited.

"No there isn't," I said. "I've been in there too."

"Have you? Well, you can't have had a proper look round, if you never saw the tunnel."

"Tunnel? What tunnel? You're making it up." But then, I remembered, Jake and I had left the place in rather a hurry. Because that was the day of the fire.

Hannah led me across the street and into the yard of the warehouse. It loomed above us, horribly dark; the partly-open doorway was darker still.

"We won't be able to see a thing in there," I muttered.

"Good thing I brought this then, isn't it?" She took a torch out of her jacket.

We went in. It was far, far scarier than the last time. The light of the torch showed only small areas of the huge room. All the rest was total blackness, as cold as a tomb.

I felt the hairs rise up on the back of my neck. When I grabbed Hannah's arm, she didn't shake me off.

"The stairs are at the far end," she whispered.

"I know."

Jake and I had explored up the stairs – we had not noticed the steps leading down. They were there, though. Hannah shone the torch on them. Darkness swooped in, and gathered behind us, and followed us down.

Oh God – help me! I'm really scared!

Leave all your worries with him, because he cares for you. He cares for you. He cares for you... It was like being lost in the mountains at night, and seeing, a long way off, the lights of a house. I felt a tiny bit more brave – I could go on.

The stairs came out near the bottom of the lift shaft.

A broad passage led off to one side. I thought it was heading in the direction of the street.

When we had gone a few paces, Hannah said, "This is as far as we got. We didn't have a torch with us, and Tanya got frightened."

"Didn't you ever come back?"

"No. Basin Street was getting overcrowded. First Mr Lewis nosing around, then Neddy and his friends. We've found someplace better now."

"Have you? Where?"

"Not telling."

The passage went on and on. "We must be underneath the street by now," I said. "I wonder why they built this tunnel?"

"To move things from one building to the other, I suppose, without getting in the way of the traffic."

"What traffic? There never is any in Basin Street."

"There would have been in the old days. Shhh!" She gripped my arm tightly.

We both stood still, and then I heard it too – the sound of a car. It passed right overhead. Not just any car: something powerful. A Ferrari?

The torchlight jumped, the shadows leapt fearfully, as we ran along the tunnel.

"Oh no! Look at that!"

Ahead of us, totally blocking the passage, was a heap of rubble. It looked as if Neddy and his friends had built a barrier out of anything they could find – old bricks, lumps of wood, bits of broken shelving, shattered doors. It filled the tunnel from floor to ceiling. There was no way through.

Chapter 19

What did one wall say to the other wall?

Meet me at the corner.

"What are you doing?" cried Hannah.

"I'm not giving up now," I said. Climbing up the heap of rubble, I started scrabbling away at it. I threw bits of wood onto the ground behind me. Half of a door slid down with a crash.

"Pass me the torch." I had made a small gap between the barrier and the ceiling. When I shone the torch through, I could see the doors of a lift. Yes! We were inside the warehouse!

I wriggled through the gap I'd made and climbed down on the other side. "Wait for me!" Hannah cried. "Don't go off and leave me in the dark!"

She crawled through the space, her face as white as paper. Hannah was scared too! For some reason this made me feel better.

"Give me back that torch. It's mine," she said.

I made for the stairs beside the lift. Suddenly something caught my foot, and I went sprawling. At the same moment I heard a bell ringing somewhere up above.

Hannah helped me get up. "Look," she said, shining the torch on the floor. "It's some kind of trip wire."

"Neddy fixed that up, I bet. Come on!"

We hurried up the stairs. I could hear other footsteps running down towards us. "Neddy!" I shouted.

A bright light shone right in my eyes. "Who's that?" said an angry voice. "What do you want?"

"We're friends of Neddy's," I gasped. "We've come – we've come to warn you. Two men from Grandfield are on their way here. They want to get you out of here."

"Oh do they? That's nothing new." But he stopped shining the torch in my face. "You'd better come up."

We followed him up two flights of stairs. "Look out," he said, "there's another trip wire just here. Neddy! Are you awake? Someone here looking for you."

We were on the upper floor by now, in a corridor. A door opened, and Neddy looked out. "I heard the alarm," he said rather sleepily. "Ben! Hannah! What are you doing here?"

As quickly as I could, I told the story. "And he could be here any time," I said. "We heard a car that might have been his."

"How was he planning to get in here?" asked the man.

"I don't know. A ladder? Ropes? Dynamite?"

"He knows his way around the warehouses," said Hannah. "I've seen him here before."

By now the man was listening intently. "And you don't know what he means to do?"

"No. But his friend said something about 'people could get hurt'."

"We'd better be ready for him," the man said. He ran down the corridor, banging on doors. "Action stations, everybody! Wake up! All hands on deck! Stand by to repel boarders!"

"That guy watches too many old war movies," said Hannah.

"Where's your grandmother?" I said to Neddy.

"She's up on the roof. It's her turn to keep watch tonight – we'd better warn her too."

He ran upstairs. Hannah and I went with him, because among all the people who were starting to mill about in the corridor – eight or ten of them – Neddy's was the only face we knew. Also, something was worrying me. If Mrs Fortescue was keeping watch up there, why hadn't she seen Hannah and me, or heard us knocking at the gate?

We found the answer when we stepped out onto the roof. Neddy's grandmother was sitting with her back to the wall, eyes closed, snoring gently.

"I *told* her she's too old for this kind of thing," said Neddy. "Grandmother! Wake up!"

Awake, she stopped being a little old lady and became Mrs Fortescue again. She quickly understood what was happening.

"Right. There are four of us," she said. "That means we can each keep watch on a different side of the building. I've always said this job is too big for one person."

Yeah. Especially if that person falls asleep… But I didn't dare to say it.

"I'll watch the front of the building," she decided. "Edward, you take the back, Ben and Hannah the two sides. But do be careful – this roof isn't at all safe. Test every step before you put your weight on it."

We followed our orders. Near the edge of the roof,

I got down on hands and knees, because there was no railing – nothing at all to stop you falling off. (I never have been all that keen on heights.) Very cautiously, lying on my stomach, I peered over. Below was the yard at the side of the warehouse, deep in shadow; then the wall, and beyond it the yard of the warehouse next door.

Would they try to get in that way? They would need ladders and wire-cutters. It would be possible, though. Or rather it would have been possible earlier, when the lookout – and everyone else – was asleep. But now, Neddy's friends were searching the yard with torches; only idiots would try to get in now.

What if they were already inside, though? What if they had been too quick for us?

"All clear this side," someone shouted down below.

"Probably a false alarm," said somebody else. "Can we go back to bed now?"

I saw the red glow as a man lit a cigarette. Funny; I could smell it all the way up here. The sound of voices came up clearly, too.

"We'd better have a couple of extra people on guard through the night." It was the man who had met us on the stairs. "Any volunteers?"

"Did anyone check the underground passage?" a woman said.

"It's blocked."

"But that's how those kids got in, isn't it?"

"What kids? I wish someone would tell me what's going on," another woman complained.

I could still smell smoke. Surely Hannah hadn't chosen this moment to have a cigarette?

All of a sudden there was the crash of breaking

glass. Directly below me, a man's head leaned out of a broken window. And a great cloud of smoke swirled up towards me.

"Fire!" the man yelled. "Help! Fire!"

Chapter 20

Which famous soldier invented the fireplace?

Alexander the Grate.

Our first thought was to get down from the roof. We all headed for the door at the top of the stairs. It was shut – and the moment I opened it, smoke burst out like a silent explosion. I stepped back, coughing and choking.

"We'll never get down there," said Neddy. "The staircase is acting just like a chimney."

"It's only smoke, not flames," Hannah said. "We could make a run for it…"

Mrs Fortescue said, "Far too dangerous. Smoke can kill faster than flames can. It gets into your lungs and suffocates you. Is there another way down?"

"There's a fire escape at the other end of the building," said Neddy. "But the steps don't come up as far as the roof."

"Better than nothing," his grandmother said. "Not so far to fall."

Fall? I didn't want to fall! There must be another way down! Frantically I looked around for a ladder, a piece of rope… anything…

"Wait a minute," said Neddy. "I don't believe this is a real fire. I think it's Mr Lewis's way of getting us out of the building."

"You think so? A smoke bomb, or something?" I said hopefully.

But Hannah said, "In that case, why did they talk about people getting hurt?"

There was no answer to that.

I crawled back to the edge of the roof. Smoke was streaming up from the windows below. Through it I could dimly see people running about in the yard. Some were moving aside the barrier that blocked the doorway into the street.

"Help! Help!" I shouted. "We're trapped on the roof!" But no one seemed to hear. And then, amidst the smoke, I saw a bright flicker of flame.

I ran back to the others. "It is a real fire," I said.

"I bet it was Lewis who started it, though," said Neddy.

Hannah cried, "Who cares who started it? Let's get out of here!"

"There's no need to panic," said Mrs Fortescue severely. "We are not in any immediate danger. The safest thing to do is simply to wait for the Fire Brigade. Which part of the building seems to be the worst affected, Ben? This end or the other end?"

"This end."

"In that case we'll move along towards the other end. But do spread out, and go carefully. Remember, this roof is quite fragile."

When she mentioned the roof, I remembered the fire in that other warehouse. Particularly, the terrible crash as the roof fell in on top of the flames. And the Fire Brigade arriving too late to save the building… Fear was gnawing away at me from the inside.

"Do you suppose anyone's called the Fire Brigade?" I whispered to Neddy.

"Oh, help. I hope so."

Some people were out in the street by now. How long would it take them to find a public phone? How long before we could hope to hear the fire engines coming?

Keeping well apart, to spread the weight, we followed Mrs Fortescue over the roof. I was the only one who didn't have a torch. But my eyes were well adjusted to the darkness – or so I thought. I was wrong.

I must have stepped onto one of the skylight windows let into the roof. It didn't break; it opened beneath me like a trap door. I dropped downwards into the darkness and smoke. There was no warning, not even time to scream.

When I hit the floor... that was when I screamed.

Oh, the pain! It felt as if both my ankles were broken. In agony I lay on the floor, hardly noticing the smoke that swirled all around me.

"Ben! Ben! Are you okay?"

"No," I groaned. "My legs..."

Above me, I could just make out three pale faces looking down. Someone was shining a torch; its light was almost swallowed up in the billowing dark clouds.

Neddy shouted, "Can you climb back up? Is there anything to stand on?"

I tried to stand up – but it hurt too much. I collapsed in a heap. Up above, they were arguing about what to do, but I hardly heard them. Nothing mattered... only the pain.

"Ben," came Neddy's voice. "Can you move over a bit? I'm coming down."

I heaved myself to one side. The torchlight shone on a pair of legs dangling through the skylight. Neddy lowered himself until he was hanging by his fingertips. Then he let go, landed lightly, and crawled over to me.

"Keep low down," he said – as if I had a choice in the matter. "Smoke rises. The air's better near the floor."

"What are we going to do?"

"We can crawl to the fire escape. It's at the far end of the corridor. Now where are we, exactly?"

He waved his torch around. The smoke seemed to be getting thicker. I could vaguely make out rows of shelves on both sides of us; beyond that I couldn't see anything at all.

Well, it could be worse. At least there were no flames in sight – not yet.

"I think we're in the biggest storeroom," said Neddy. "We need to find the door into the corridor. But which way is it?" He started to cough, and I remembered about his asthma. The smoke wouldn't do him any good at all.

"Can you manage to crawl?" he gasped. "I think it's this way."

I dragged myself along on hands and knees. The pain was horrific. Keep going – keep going –

After a lifetime or two, we came to the end of the row of shelves. There was a gap, and then the wall of the room. Neddy shone his torch to right and left, but in the thickening smoke it was almost useless.

"I can't... see the door," he gasped. His voice sounded wheezy. "There is only one. Which way?"

Oh, God! What do we do now? Help us... please help us...

Neddy, making his mind up, pointed to the left. "Let's try this way."

No. Go to the right.

The voice was so clear, at first I thought there was someone in the room with us. "Did you hear that?" I said to Neddy.

"Hear what?"

"Somebody telling us to go to the right."

"Okay then." He didn't have the breath to argue, which was just as well, because by now I wasn't sure if I'd imagined it.

Turning right meant we were heading back towards the source of the fire. The torch was no good at all. Smoke blinded us with tears, made us cough and choke, made our lungs feel like a chimney blocked with soot.

I felt my way along the base of the wall. It was never-ending. I had made a mistake – I had imagined that voice. We must be heading away from the door; we would never find it. We would die here, by this endless wall…

Then, reaching out, my hand found a space. The doorway!

"Which way now?"

"Left," Neddy wheezed. "Along the corridor."

Was it imagination, or did the floor feel warm beneath me? And what was that sound – the crackle of flames?

By now Neddy was in a worse state than I was. "Don't wait for me," he gasped.

"No. Come on, Neddy! It can't be far now!"

I forgot the pain in my ankles. I forgot everything except our goal. What if, when we reached the fire door, I couldn't open it? No, don't think about that. Just keep moving…

And there it was at last – the open doorway. With the last of our strength, we dragged ourselves out onto the fire escape. I felt the cold metal under my hands. I breathed the beautiful, cool, clean air. I heard the rising wail of a fire engine – the best, the loveliest sound in the whole world.

Chapter 21

Doctor, doctor, I can't get to sleep at night.

Well, lie at the very edge of the bed and you'll soon drop off.

I don't remember much about the rescue operation. Well, I didn't actually see much of it. I saw the shoulder of the firefighter who carried me down the steps. I saw Neddy, slumped in the arms of another fireman. Then there was an ambulance… and then I don't remember any more, until I woke up in hospital with both my feet in plaster.

Mum and Dad were by my bed. It looked as if Mum had been crying; Dad had his arm around her.

"Where's Neddy?" I croaked.

Mum couldn't speak. She started crying again, and a terrible fear hit me.

"Where's Neddy? Is he all right?"

"Neddy's fine," said Dad rather hoarsely. "Look – there he is."

I saw that Neddy was in the next bed to mine. He had lost his glasses; without them his face looked strange, sort of defenceless. And he was very pale. But he waved to me; he was all right.

"What about Hannah? And Mrs Fortescue?"

"Safe at home. The fire brigade got them down from the roof just in time," said Dad.

"It was a miracle nobody got killed," said Mum shakily. "But what about you, love? How are you feeling?"

"Not too bad," I said, although my lungs felt clogged with soot, and my feet were still throbbing with pain. At least, I assumed they were my feet, those things that looked like ski-boots with my toes sticking out of the ends.

I had damaged my legs again – the second time in a year. And this looked much worse than the injury from last winter's Fun Run. This could mean no football for months.

But it didn't matter. We were all safe – nothing else mattered.

"What I want to know is, why were you up on a warehouse roof at that time of night?" said Dad.

"Shhh," said Mum. "That can wait."

They were sitting really close together – closer than they had been for weeks. And they were both staring at me. I felt quite embarrassed.

I said, "How did you get on in Southampton, Dad?"

"Southampton?" For a moment Dad sounded almost as mystified as Grandad. "Oh – jobs, you mean. No, I didn't find anything. But right at this moment I couldn't care less. I'm just thankful that you're all right, son."

When Mum and Dad had gone, Neddy came over to see me.

"Thanks," I said rather awkwardly.

"What for?"

"Saving my life, of course."

"Oh, it was nothing," he said.

"My life is nothing? Thanks very much."

He said, "Anyway, it was you that got us out. But I still don't understand how you found the way to the door."

"I told you – I heard this voice saying go to the right. Who was it? One of your friends?"

"No. They got out by the fire escape as soon as they had raised the alarm. And it wasn't Grandmother or Hannah, because they didn't have a clue where we were."

"Who, then?"

There was only one possible answer.

Neddy went home the next day. But I wasn't lonely; I had loads of visitors. Grandad came, bringing me some Mars Bars and a brand new joke book. I told him everything that had happened.

"Do you think I really did get a message from God?" I asked him.

"Very likely. But was that the only time you heard God's voice that night?"

"What do you mean?"

"Didn't you ever stop to think, as you went out of the house late at night, that it might not be the right thing to do? That you were breaking the rules your Dad had set? That it might all go horribly wrong?"

Oh no, not another lecture. (I had already had a huge telling-off from Mum and Dad, once they knew for certain that I was going to be okay.)

"We just didn't think," I told Grandad. "We were in too much of a hurry. But earlier on… yes, I suppose I did get the feeling that I shouldn't be doing this. It was when I was trying to get into the flat."

"That might have been God's voice too, you know," said Grandad. "That feeling of shouldn't-be-doing-this. The Bible says, *If you wander off the road to the right or the left, you will hear his voice behind you saying, 'Here is the road. Follow it.'* Now that's not talking about when you're trapped in a smoke-filled room. That means all the everyday choices you make about what you're going to do."

I thought about this. Maybe he was right, and yet…

"I didn't listen," I said. "I knew it wasn't really the right thing, but I went ahead. And what if I hadn't? If I hadn't overheard Mr Lewis, we wouldn't have been able to warn Neddy and his friends."

"Who knows what would have happened?" said Grandad. "Only God knows that. But perhaps your warning made very little difference. Perhaps everyone would still have got out safely without your help."

"And perhaps I wouldn't be lying here, missing the start of the football season," I said gloomily.

"That's true. But the great thing is, God doesn't give up on us. He loves us too much for that."

"Even when we go wrong?"

"Yes. We do make mistakes; we're only human. But we can always come back to him. We can still hear his voice, if we listen for it, saying *Here is the road. Follow it.*"

Hannah came to visit me, too. She brought me some grapes – I hate grapes. But that didn't matter because by the time she left, most of them were gone.

She was in a strange mood, not talking much. There

was something on her mind. Eventually she came out with it.

"Ben, I'm sorry. I should have been the one who came to rescue you – not Neddy."

"Why?" I said, surprised. "You didn't know your way around the building. He was the one who knew about the fire escape."

"Yes, but I'm older than him, and I don't have asthma. And I am your sister. I knew it should have been me… but I was scared."

"We were all scared," I said. "Neddy was, too."

"But he still went in. It was like he got extra courage from somewhere."

"From God, maybe," I said, and waited for her to argue back. But she didn't. Instead, she quickly changed the subject.

"Hey, have you heard about Mr Lewis? He's been arrested!"

"What?"

"Yeah. Last night. The police came to the flat and took him away."

"Do they know he was the one who started the fire?"

"I've no idea. The problem is, we can't prove anything, can we? You could tell the police what you heard, but it would only be your word against his. He would deny everything."

"Perhaps they found a clue. He dropped his wallet, or something, at the scene of the crime," I said hopefully.

"That sort of thing only happens in books. But they're certainly taking a close look at how the fire started. You can't get near Basin Street for police."

Not for the first time, I wished I wasn't trapped in bed, missing all the action.

Hannah said, "Greg's got this theory. He thinks Lewis could have set light to that heap of rubbish in the tunnel – you know, the barrier we climbed over – so the smoke would go up the staircase. But then the fire spread and got out of hand. Greg also thinks Lewis could have started that other warehouse fire a few weeks ago."

"Why? To speed up the demolition of Basin Street?"

"Maybe. Or maybe he's like Greg – fond of fires. Greg says –"

"You seem really keen on Greg," I said. "You're not going out with him, are you?"

"I might be," she said, looking smug. "But don't worry, little brother. He won't be starting any more fires, not while I'm around. I never want to smell smoke again as long as I live."

And now, six weeks later, it's the day for my plaster casts to come off. My feet have been covered up for six weeks. Phew! I'm not sure I want to be in the same room with them when they are unwrapped.

A lot has happened in six weeks. Most important, Mr Lewis is in prison, waiting to go to trial.

"How did the police catch up with him?" I asked Jake.

"I don't know. I expect it will all come out at the trial. Some people say it was his assistant who went to the police. You know – the guy who helped him start the fire."

"Why would he do that?"

"Because he was shocked by what happened. He

didn't want to put anyone's life in danger, just scare them a bit."

"Yes," I said, remembering the conversation I'd overheard. "But Lewis didn't care if people got hurt or not. He seemed to think they deserved it, for getting in his way."

"I hope they put Lewis away for a long time," said Jake.

Everyone knew who Lewis was working for. After the fire, Grandfield became a dirty word in Westhaven. The Town Council refused to sign a deal with them – so the marina project is dead in the water. The Council are looking for other ways to use the land at Basin Street. A caravan park? A sports hall? Housing for old people?

"Dreadful, dreadful," says Miss Grindlay. "Horrible ideas, all of them. Destroying the unique atmosphere of the town."

"I don't care what they do," says Neddy, "as long as they leave the Basin alone."

I don't care what they do, full stop. For Dad has found work at last! He's helping to build a new hotel at Barcliff. He says it's a good sign – new buildings going up mean the recession could be coming to an end.

We've got different people living in the downstairs flat, a couple with a young baby. The baby cries a lot. Dad says he should have soundproofed the flat, because every time the baby cries, Jerry starts barking. (Unfortunately there's no way of soundproofing Jerry.)

It's my birthday next week; I'll be twelve. And I have

made a sort of New Year Resolution. Wait for it – I'm going to stop telling jokes.

Why? Well, when I was in hospital, there was this doctor. Dr Vincent. I liked him at first because he was always joking around. But then, after a while, he began to get on my nerves. And I wasn't the only person who felt like that. I noticed the nurses would sort of flinch when Dr Vincent breezed into the ward, scattering jokes around like machine-gun bullets, and braying with laughter.

"What an idiot that doctor is," I said to Jake, who was eating the last of my grapes.

"You think so? Then be warned. That could be you in twenty years' time."

"I'm not as bad as that," I protested. "I don't tell jokes *all* the time. Anyway, I could stop if I wanted to."

"Bet you couldn't."

"Bet I could."

"How much?"

"I bet you a fiver that I could go for a month without telling a single joke."

"Okay. You're on."

"I'll start on my birthday," I said.

But that's not until next week. So here's one last joke for you:

This is an announcement for passengers travelling to London Euston. The train now approaching platforms 4,5,6,7,8,9 and 10 is coming in sideways.

Oh, you've heard it before? Oops… Sorry.